**KA-**

D0978569

The third time he started past, the strange rider stopped, facing Longarm's back, and looked both ways, more than once, before his gun hand dropped to the grips of that Schofield, even as their eyes met in the mirror.

The stranger, intent on shooting Longarm in the back, seeing he was in for it now, like it or not, drew as if his very life depended on it. For it did, just as Longarm's life depended on beating the son of a bitch to the draw!

Whirling off his stool, Longarm threw that mug of black coffee in his free hand as he went for his own gun with the other in the slow, dreamy process of dropping to the walk on his right side and shoulder as they both fired.

Then, seeing he still seemed able, Longarm fired again, then again in the space of less than two full seconds, as he sprawled on the walk in a confusion of earsplitting gunshots and eye-blinding gun smoke. While he tried to figure out what in blue blazes he was doing, even as he just kept doing it . . .

## DON'T MISS THESE
## ALL-ACTION WESTERN SERIES
## FROM THE BERKLEY PUBLISHING GROUP

**THE GUNSMITH by J. R. Roberts**
Clint Adams was a legend among lawmen, outlaws, and ladies. They called him . . . the Gunsmith.

**LONGARM by Tabor Evans**
The popular long-running series about U.S. Deputy Marshal Long—his life, his loves, his fight for justice.

**SLOCUM by Jake Logan**
Today's longest-running action Western. John Slocum rides a deadly trail of hot blood and cold steel.

**BUSHWHACKERS by B. J. Lanagan**
An action-packed series by the creators of Longarm! The rousing adventures of the most brutal gang of cutthroats ever assembled—Quantrill's Raiders.

**DIAMONDBACK by Guy Brewer**
Dex Yancey is Diamondback, a southern gentleman turned con man when his brother cheats him out of the family fortune. Ladies love him. Gamblers hate him. But nobody pulls one over on Dex . . .

**WILDGUN by Jack Hanson**
Will Barlow's continuing search for his daughter, kidnapped by the Blackfeet Indians who slaughtered the rest of his family.

## TABOR EVANS

# LONGARM

### AND THE MAD BOMBER'S BRIDE

JOVE BOOKS, NEW YORK

This is a work of fiction. Names, characters, places, and incidents are either the product of the author's imagination or are used fictitiously, and any resemblance to actual persons, living or dead, business establishments, events, or locales is entirely coincidental.

LONGARM AND THE MAD BOMBER'S BRIDE

A Jove Book / published by arrangement with
the author

PRINTING HISTORY
Jove edition / December 2000

The Penguin Putnam Inc. World Wide Web site address is
http://www.penguinputnam.com

ISBN: 0-515-12977-1

A JOVE BOOK®
Jove Books are published by The Berkley Publishing Group,
a division of Penguin Putnam Inc.,
375 Hudson Street, New York, New York 10014.
JOVE and the "J" design
are trademarks belonging to Penguin Putnam Inc.

PRINTED IN THE UNITED STATES OF AMERICA

10  9  8  7  6  5  4  3  2  1

# Chapter 1

As a man who packed a badge and a .44-40, U.S. Deputy Marshal Custis Long of the Denver District Court had his own reservations about the institution of marriage. But when he first laid eyes on Miss Clovinia Cullpepper of South Carolina, he became convinced of the madness of Professor Norman MacLennon. For while any man might entertain second thoughts about signing away his rights to a night out with the boys, nobody but a raving lunatic could have written such a nasty letter to such a vision of honey-blond loveliness.

He found her waiting for him, as they'd said she'd be, in a room off the lobby of the Tremont House near Colfax and Broadway, across from the Overland Stagecoach Terminal on the edge of Downtown Denver. The Tremont House had seen better days. But lots of newcomers who'd come in by stage from Julesberg wound up staying there.

So Longarm, as he was better known to friend and foe alike, used the musty atmosphere of the somewhat seedy Tremont House as a more graceful opening than, say, "What's this I hear about your betrothed throwing you over for a mining camp madam?"

As the honey-blond vision in summer-weight blue silk

1

that matched her red-rimmed eyes rose to extend a hand to him, Longarm began by asking her to call him Custis instead of "Good sir," and added, "The Palace down by the Union Depot or that new Dexter Hotel a tad closer might be more suited to a lady of quality for the time you mean to stay in these parts, ma'am."

Sitting back down and patting a space on the settee beside her, she gracefully replied, "*My* friends call me Clo, Custis. To make no bones about it, I've priced other hotels here in Denver and since I don't know how long I may have to stay out here, I have to take such practical matters under consideration."

Longarm sat down beside her to politely ask, "How come? Meaning no disrespect to your tracking abilities, Miss Clo, my boss, Marshal Billy Vail, allows the War Department in Washington has taken almost as great an interest in the odd behavior of your intended as you've had every right to. So my orders are to get on down to the New Mexico Territory and see what seems to be eating him."

She bitterly replied, "He says her name is Claudette and he's with her in the city of Gilead in the Sangre de Cristo Mountains."

To which Longarm soberly replied, "That wide spot in the trail they call Gilead hardly qualifies as a city, Miss Clo, and after that, we don't know for certain he's still there. I know he sent you a right nasty hate letter from there. But it's been my experience that once a man sends a mess of hate mail that includes President Hayes and that new Federal Governor of New Mexico, Lew Wallace, he's inclined to move it on down the road. I'll naturally commence scouting for sign down Gilead way, and I mean to get right to it. I know you're anxious, and so is the Secretary of War. But we thought it best if I interviewed you some about the professor. Before he commenced to behave so unusual, even for him. I understand that during

2

the war he made gunpowder for the Army of Virginia from . . . unusual supplies?"

The well-bred but self-confessed pragmatist made no bones about that either as she demurely replied, "Outhouse scrapings, or the crystals of potassium nitrate one can leach from the urine-soaked earth of such . . . facilities. A lot of people thought Norman was a bit unusual when he first proposed the idea. But there were a lot of outhouses, stable yards, and such in Dixie, so . . ."

"Professor MacLennon wasn't the only chemistry teacher who noticed that, Miss Clo," Longarm politely noted. "Any chemist can tell you saltpeter, or potassium nitrate, is a natural waste product as well as the most important ingredient of gunpowder. A lot of Confederate gunpowder started out a mite disgusting. What has Washington worried is how your Professor MacLennon made so *much* of it, with such raw material as he had to work with."

Resisting the urge to reach for a smoke in the same stuffy room he was sharing with a lady of quality, Longarm soberly added, "Lots of unreconstructed rebels write letters threatening to blow public figures out of bed one fine morning. But not too many of them seem to be chemistry professors known to be experts on the subject of explosives, high and low. In his threatening letter to Governor Lew Wallace, your Norman makes mention of nitroglycerine, and I have been given to understand you commence with the nitric acid any high school chemistry student would be familiar with. I know how to make glycerine my ownself. You render it from beef suet down in Butcher Town by the Burlington yards. They make fancy soap out of glycerine—when they ain't out to blow the Governor of New Mexico out of bed, that is."

She allowed she just didn't understand what could have gotten into her sometimes remote but hitherto loving Norman.

Longarm mused half to himself, "They say old Lew Wallace was this Union general during the war. But there are greater Union generals still with us, and Governor Wallace says nothing about the war at all in that thick book he just published about Mr. Ben Hur. Did you ever hear your intended make mention of General Wallace—or, for that matter, President Hayes—before he just up and lit out on you from Charleston, Miss Clo?"

She sniffed and sighed. "He never said a word to anyone before he simply, as you put it, lit out on us all. He said not a word about leaving his chemistry students in mid-term. He never said a word to his housekeeper, and his faithful body servant doesn't think he even packed one traveling bag. One morning he was simply gone, and we were worried sick until his spiteful letters from New Mexico Territory began to arrive, postmarked from a place you describe as a rather out-of-the-way hamlet."

"Mining camp, Miss Clo," he said, correcting her. "Gilead ain't half quaint enough to call a hamlet."

He started to tell her what a smelly little place Gilead had been that one time he'd ridden through. He decided not to, and settled for fishing out his pocket watch and observing, "No offense, but I have to get cracking if I'm to pick up my travel orders and catch a southbound combination leaving well this side of sundown, Miss Clo. It's up to you whether to head on home or wait out here for word. But it could take us a spell if he's lit out from Gilead, with or without the lady he mentioned to you so spitefully."

As they both rose, he said, "I don't suppose he mentioned anyone else we might want to talk to?"

She shook her head and replied, "Not out this way." Then she shot a thoughtful frown up at him and added, "There *was* one puzzling thing about that letter I allowed your superior, Marshal Vail, to file. I'd have to read it over to recall the exact details, of course. But Norman did

4

make mention, quite unpleasantly, of my old beau, Sam, and suggested I . . . ah, join him at some address on Jeremiah Street. But I never had an old beau named Sam, and there's no Jeremiah Street in Charleston."

Longarm shrugged and said, "Well, we know he seems confused of late. A jealous heart sees old beaus where others might not. Don't you have any casual acquaintances named Sam, Miss Clo?"

She shook her head. "None that fit the cryptic remarks in Norman's letter of renunciation. He distinctly orders me to report to Sam at such and such a number on Jeremiah Street and tell him he was right all along. But I've simply no idea who this Sam might be or what Sam could be right or wrong about!"

Longarm allowed he couldn't make much sense of the suggestion either, and ticked his hat brim to her as he said, "I'll tell them at the office you'll be staying here for now, Miss Clo. They might be able to work something better out for you, if they can't talk you into heading back East. But I have to be going now if I'm to go anywhere important this evening."

They shook on it and parted friendly. Outside in the afternoon sunlight, Longarm headed north along Denver's version of Broadway, catching occasional glimpses of himself in the plate-glass windows of some bigger stores along the way. There was nothing he could do about the infernal three-piece suit of tobacco tweed a fussy reform Administration expected federal employees to wear on duty in town these days. Things had been far more corrupt but a lot more comfortable back when President Grant and his own political cronies had been running the country, even if some of them had tried to ride the country into the ground.

But at least President Hayes and his First Lady, Lemonade Lucy, had listened to reason when it came to pancaked coffee-brown Stetsons, stovepipe army boots, and a double-action Colt .44-40 discreetly worn cross-draw under the tweed tails of his frock coat, Longarm thought as he ambled on over to the Denver Federal Building.

He mounted the marble stairway inside to the second floor, where the office suite of Marshal William Vail discreetly squatted behind one oaken door along the long corridor.

Inside, he found young Henry, the pale-faced kid who played their typewriter, stuffing onionskin travel orders in a hemp-paper envelope. Henry told Longarm their boss wanted a word with him before he headed out into the field. So Longarm ambled back to the oak-paneled inner sanctum of the bearish Marshal Billy Vail.

One would hardly know it looking at him now, but in his own days in the field a younger and surely slimmer Billy Vail had ridden with the Texas Rangers after Comanches, Mexican raiders, and far worse owlhoot riders than they grew nowadays. To hear him tell it at least. But now Vail was just older and far shorter and fatter than his senior deputy.

As if he'd been brooding about this, Billy Vail frowned up from behind his cluttered desk and demanded, "Well, what might you have got out of that Carolina gal about her mad bomber?"

Longarm sat uninvited in the one horsehair-padded leather chair on his side of the desk, and reached for a three-for-a-nickel cheroot as he calmly replied, "She's a lady of quality and I like her. I tried to get her to go on home and let us worry about the shiftless skunk who broke her heart. I don't expect she will, and she might take it wrong if I offered to let her stay in my quarters whilst I'm out of town."

Vail grudgingly replied, "My old woman's already ahead of you, and a lady of quality might still be able to hold her head up when she leaves if she spends her nights in Denver up to our place on Sherman Street. You know

6

you're going to have to kill the crazy son of a bitch, of course."

Longarm thumbnailed a match aflame to light his cheroot and give himself time to choose his words before he calmly replied, "I'm paid to ride as a lawman, not a public executioner. It has to be against some federal law to threaten government officials with nitroglycerine bombs. So, do I catch up with Professor MacLennon, I mean to arrest him and bring him in alive, if he'll let me. If he makes me kill him, I will. But don't you ever *order* me to kill anybody again, and I ain't fixing to say that more than once!"

Billy Vail said soothingly, "Don't get your bowels in an uproar, old son. I only meant it looks as if you're going to have to kill the maniac because he's sworn he'll never be taken alive and has surrounded himself with high explosives down Gilead way."

Longarm took a long-overdue drag on his cheroot, blew a thoughtful smoke ring, and stared at his boss through the smoke ring as he flatly stated, "I don't expect to find Norman MacLennon in Gilead. Would you stay in a dinky town after sending out a flood of threatening letters by way of the one post office for a day's ride in any direction?"

To which Vail replied easily, "I'm not a mad bomber. He is. He was *loco en la cabeza* to send such spiteful warnings to begin with. No mad bomber with a lick of common sense would warn folks in advance he was out to blow them up. He'd just blow them up without a word of warning, right?"

Longarm gently pointed out, "A mad bomber with a lick of common sense sounds like a contradiction in terms. But I follow your drift, and I *said* I'd start scouting for sign in Gilead. I just don't expect to find him there, either surrounded by high explosives or just jerking off."

"He's there," Billy Vail insisted, waving a yellow tele-

7

graph form as he explained. "This just came back from a barkeep I wired down to Gilead. He's there and hanging out with a noisy crowd of unreconstructed rebels I've sent other queries out on. That Madam Claudette he wrote Miss Clovinia about is well known in the Sangre de Cristos as a whore who'll take it three ways for three dollars, and her parlor house is running wide-open, day and night, across from the rendering plant. You knew they tanned hides and rendered tallow Mexican-style down yonder in Gilead, didn't you?"

Longarm grimaced and dryly asked, "Who could forget such a sickly sweet stench?"

He felt no call to lecture an older Texican on how the Mexicans had commenced the Western cattle industry their own way, raising longhorn Hispano-Moorish stock for hides and tallow rather than its stringy beef. Left to their druthers, Spanish-speaking folks preferred chicken or pork to even the best beef. So that was how Spanish cordovan leather, castile soap, and perfumed tallow candles had gotten to be so popular in other parts. When Vail mentioned the narrow-gauge line from Gilead to the capital in Santa Fe, Longarm nodded and allowed they'd been building it when he'd passed through.

He said, "Seems to me they'd just opened up some sort of mine down yonder. It was likely the ore they wanted to carry by rail out to the rest of the world."

Vail sounded serious, even for him, when he soberly replied, "It's the mine the War Department is so hot and bothered about. They've been thinking of setting it aside as a strategic reserve."

Longarm smiled uncertainly and declared, "I give up. Are we talking about a whole lot of copper or a whole lot of lead down yonder?"

Vail shook his bullet head and answered simply, "Bat shit. Tons and tons of bat shit deposited in miles of caves under the Sangre de Cristo rimrocks in the past million years or so. Since striking such a lode, they've been shipping crude bat guano as fertilizer. But fertilizer's not what the War Department is so hot and bothered about, see?"

Longarm saw indeed, and whistled in wonder as he considered how much nitroglycerine a high school chemistry student could whip up with an unlimited supply of longhorn tallow and a mountain range filled with bat shit laced with potassium nitrate!

Then he rose to his considerable height and declared, "I'd best get on down to Gilead and put a stop to all this . . . bat shit!"

# Chapter 2

It seemed a crying shame. But in his six or eight years with the Justice Department, Longarm had learned a lot of folks lied when the truth was in their favor. So, knowing in advance he'd likely need to check out some records, Longarm went first to where such records were kept, the territorial capital at Santa Fe, a tad west of the bat-shit-contaminated Sierra Sangre de Cristos.

Getting to Santa Fe from Denver wasn't easy. Founded by Spaniards out of Mexico to the south near the head-waters of the Rio Grande ten years before the Pilgrims found Plymouth Rock, Santa Fe still seemed easier to get to from Mexico. You only had to follow the river and newer railroad tracks due north from El Paso. Coming down from Denver, you had to switchback over mountain passes until you took to wondering if such a trip would be worth it even if they had the Pearly Gates awaiting for you, wide-open, at the end of the damned line.

But as all things good and bad must, Longarm's tedious and grimy ordeal by rail finally ended with him standing on an open platform in the considerably cooler shades of evening at the altitude of Santa Fe. So he ambled on over to the Posada con Vista Linda, and hired a room to turn in early and go over all the paperwork Henry had saddled him with in that one fat envelope.

Old Henry, for all his prissy ways, was a hard-riding fool on that typewriting machine. So he'd transcribed all the letters posted from nearby Gilead by Professor Norman MacLennon, and this was just as well, because it would have been harder to read such ravings in the original longhand. They read mighty wild in Henry's neatly typed transcripts.

Longarm got out his notebook and a pencil stub, trimmed the bedside lamp's wick as bright as he could, and got undressed to prop himself bare-ass atop the covers while he searched for anything at all worth following up on.

The professor sure gave President Hayes holy hell about current Reconstruction Policy, threatening to blow such a Damnyankee trash white and his Lemonade Lucy sky high, along with a White House they'd made unfit for human habitation.

Just what this was supposed to do for the Lost Cause wasn't too clear to Longarm. For say what you would about the disputed election of Rutherford B. Hayes, and about his handsome but straitlaced First Lady serving nothing stronger than lemonade at state dinners. The current President had nevertheless used his credentials as a war hero to set aside the last Reconstruction regulations most Southerners had been bitching about. Former Confederate officers were allowed to vote, and even hold public office of late. The detested Texas State Police had been replaced by the restored and beloved Texas Rangers. So it sure beat all when Professor Norman MacLennon, a scientist who'd never been in uniform or within ten miles of any firing line, declared his intent to finish the job begun by John Wilkes Booth and maybe level the new Capitol dome as well!

His threatening letter to Governor Lew Wallace was

more personal if not one lick more sensible. It appeared the professor was still sore about a former Union officer's honorable but not outstanding military career, didn't like the way he'd been misruling New Mexico Territory, and didn't think much of that book the Governor had just had published about Mr. Ben Hur's adventures in days of yore before the war.

Longarm had heard Governor Wallace was an old army pal of President Hayes. Presidents hardly ever appointed gents they hated to political office. But as in the case of the President himself, General Wallace had just done a fair job, and anyone with a lick of sense could see the war would have ended about the same way if neither of them had ever worn a stitch of Union blue. Neither had forced Lee to surrender.

As for the way Lew Wallace had governed New Mexico, for the short time he'd been out this way, most New Mexicans seemed to feel Wallace was one hell of an improvement over the Santa Fe Ring the President had sent him to tidy up after. Some New Mexico Na-déné were out on the warpath under Victorio at the moment. But nobody blamed Governor Wallace for that. He'd put out the last smoldering embers of that Lincoln Country War by offering pardons to the survivors of both sides, and while some said young Henry or Billy the Kid was still stealing stock along the Pecos, there wasn't anybody left on the Murphy-Dolan side for him drygulch, so what the hell.

As for that book, in two illustrated volumes, Longarm had found *Ben Hur* fast-moving enough to keep a man awake in bed, and they said Lew Wallace had spent some time in the Holy Land on a diplomatic mission, which was likely where he got the notion to write about such doings.

But to hear a Carolina chemistry teacher tell it, Lew Wallace had things all wrong. MacLennon's exact words

13

on that subject read, "For a man setting himself up as biblical scholar, you certainly have a lot to learn. You don't know Saint Thomas from a pillar of salt! Ask your Papist friends at the Church of Jeremiah if that's not literally correct!"

Longarm read that passage over thrice before he decided it made no sense. It hadn't been that long since he'd read that recent novel by Governor Wallace, and Longarm was good at names. But he wrote down Saint Thomas and Church of Jeremiah for later. At the moment he just couldn't recall any mention of Saint Thomas in that book, and he'd have to ask around town in the morning if they had a . . . Church of Jeremiah?

He searched through the onionskins for the transcript of the nasty letter Miss Clovinia Cullpepper had received from the same source.

It was more personally nasty than the others. Longarm caught his jaw muscles tightening as he skimmed over the French lessons and Greek loving the poor gal's intended had taunted her with. Then Longarm got to the part he was more interested in, and sure enough, just as the pretty little thing had told him in Denver, her Norman advised her to go and get laid by some cuss named Sam at 822 Jeremiah in Charleston.

Longarm wrote that down too as he muttered, "Somebody by the name of Jeremiah done him wrong. Or he *thinks* a Jeremiah done him wrong!"

The same name cropped up again in a less spiteful but downright crazy letter addressed to President Robert E. Lee of the University of Virginia.

Crazy because, to begin with, a heartsick and ailing Robert E. Lee had only acted as a postwar college president for a short time before he'd up and died back in '70. But here was a former civilian official of the Confederacy addressing Robert E. Lee as if he was not only still alive, but itching for another go-round with those

14

Black Republican Mother Fuckers, as they were delicately described.

In his letter to Lee, MacLennon explained what a truly swamping bomb, on wheels, one could fashion from a railroad tank car filled very slowly and gently from one end with glycerine and from the other with chilled nitric acid. He allowed there'd be no call to stir the mixture as one rolled the car toward its intended target very, very gently. Longarm knew just enough high school chemistry to sense you'd want to move a tank car full of nitroglycerine even slower than that, on mighty smooth tracks!

The obviously mad bomber's letter chortled, "One of this simple but effective device's best features is that, unlike most infernal machines, this one requires neither fuses nor detonators. My crew will of course move the tank car into position fully topped to avoid the least sloshing. Nitroglycerine is fairly safe to transport in full containers. As they release the rolling bomb on a downgrade for its final roll into town, they shall of course open a tap and allow a certain amount of the highly explosive liquid to drain out, leaving space along the top of the tank car for a good hard slosh when the rolling weapon hits the end of the tracks. One slosh should do it. But, of course, for every action there is a reaction, and that much explosive liquid, the consistency of olive oil, should slosh back and forth as many times as it might take until the resulting explosion levels an area of at least a quarter-section, or let us say, five city blocks. I suggest you ask Jeremiah in the chemistry department for the exact figures. I feel sure he'll say I have it right!"

Longarm snapped his fingers and muttered, "*Transferral!* That's what them brain doctors who study maniacs in Vienna Town called it in that book about maniacs I read!"

Underlining the name Jeremiah in his notebook, Longarm went on muttering out loud. "He ain't sore at the

President or the Governor or even poor little Clovinia Cullpepper! He's pissed off fit to bust at this Jeremiah cuss he *should* be writing to! Only, being he's *loco en la cabeza* and likely teched as well, he don't *know* or won't *face* the simple fact that it's this Jeremiah cuss he'd really like to blow to Kingdom Come! So now we have to find out who Jeremiah is before the mad bomber levels a quarter-section of Charleston, Santa Fe, or Washington— if his innocent intended victims get lucky!"

Longarm set the notes and transcripts aside, but let the bed lamp be as he stared up at the herringboned willow lath and pine beams of the low ceiling, idly wondering how far this *posada* would have to be from a tank car filled with nitroglycerine when it went off. He doubted he was more than a furlong from the Santa Fe railroad yards, and such thoughts made the thick 'dobe wall between hither and yon seem thinner than it had first appeared. Most of Downtown Santa Fe was built of 'dobe, left over from before the Mexican War.

"This has to be the intended target!" Longarm decided once he'd had time to reflect on the odds of transporting a tank car filled with anything unobserved as far as Charleston, Washington, or even Denver. But a mad bomber with all that beef tallow and bat shit to start with might be able to fill a railroad tank car with nitroglycerine and set it in motion down the long narrow-gauge grade from the foothills of the nearby Sangre de Cristos. And a bomb that size going off in the middle of a town made out of glorified mud pies was not such a pretty picture to contemplate!

So he was tempted to get back up and ride, but he knew hounds who chased their own tails in circles seldom caught any rabbits. So that inspired him to sit tight and go through those territorial files by the cold light of day, and before the night was over Longarm was glad he was such a patient Christian.

Her name was Consuela, and he naturally thought she was someone from downstairs when she tapped gently on his hired door a tad after midnight. So he went to the door with just a towel wrapped around his bare ass, holding his .44-40 in the other hand just in case.

So they both felt a little awkward when he opened up and she slid in as if afraid nosy neighbors might notice. Downstairs in the cantina, castanets were clicking, high heels were clacking, and a guitar was strumming fit to bust. For Spanish-speaking folks kept late hours in the sunny climes they were attracted to. But the petite *mestiza* in a gathered black skirt and off-the-shoulder white blouse confided that she'd waited downstairs until everyone was paying attention to that Andalusian flamenco dancer before she'd risked a discreet dash up for to join him on the sly.

Since it had been her notion to shut the door after her, Longarm threw the wrought-iron bolt and led the way over to the bedstead in order to put his revolver back in its holster, draped over an oaken knobbed bedpost. As he did so, he allowed he was sorry to say he'd had no call to stock up on grub and refreshments while walking over from the depot after dark.

Consuela produced a jug of *pulque* and a poke of tostadas from under her skirt and sat on his bed, uninvited, to confide she'd been told he'd come straight over from the tracks.

So he sat down beside her, reaching for the thick glass tumblers beside the water pitcher on the bed table as he quietly asked just who might have been watching anybody that close.

As she poured, the Indian-dark but Spanish-featured *mestiza* smiled and said, "Others of La Causa, El Brazo Largo. Friends in Denver wired you were on your way here. Was not hard for to put two and two together after that, no?"

He accepted some *pulque,* but said, "No. I keep trying to tell your rebel pals I ride for the U.S. Justice Department and have standing orders not to overthrow the government of Los Estados Unidos de Mejico if it can possibly be avoided. I have brushed in the past, and I'll likely brush in the future, with *los rurales,* as Mexico's answer to the Texas Rangers call themselves. But that's simply because *los rurales* ride for El Presidente Diaz. Who's slowly working himself up to a horn-fly maggot after starting out as a graveyard worm. I ain't got nothing personal against the worthless cuss, if only he'd leave me and my friends alone."

Consuela rubbed against him like a friendly cat as she purred, "*Sí,* is well known among my people how you and some Mexican friends wiped out that artillery column over in the Baja. For who will you be riding south with this time, El Brazo Largo?"

He sipped his *pulque.* He was commencing to need it, even though it was an acquired taste indeed.

*Pulque* was to tequila as beer was to whiskey, although it was hardly the "cactus beer" some called it. Mexicans brewed regular beer. They called it *cerveza,* and it tasted about the way beer was expected to, and sometimes better. *Pulque* was the fermented but undistilled product of the same agave or century plant juice you made tequila out of. The lukewarm piss-colored contents of Consuela's jug were a slight, if only a slight, improvement over your own spit at such thirsty times. There wasn't enough alcohol in the home brew to becloud Longarm's sense of duty. So he gently but firmly told the tempting little thing, "I ain't down this way to aid and abet no *revolución,* so, no offense, you're barking up the wrong tree and I just can't use any help from you and your own rebel pals."

She looked so hurt he felt obliged to explain, "They've sent me to track down one of my own kind. He's an *hombre muy malo* who's out to kill all sorts of folks, yours,

18

mine, and any Indians selling baskets within blocks of the railroad yards. So thanks for the cheer and do you leave before that music stops downstairs, nobody down yonder will ever be the wiser. I got a long ride ahead of me to the mountains come *mañana,* hear?"

Consuela rose with a resigned expression, saying, "Some said that might be why El Brazo Largo had returned. Which one of them might you be after in that gringo mining camp? Is it the famous robber of banks or that *bombadero loco* mixing all that *mierda* in the toolshed of that house of shame?"

Longarm blinked, smiled up at her, and suddenly decided, "Hold on. Don't leave just yet, Señorita! We might have things to study on after all, if I am correct in translating *bombadero loco* to *mad bomber!*"

So Consuela squealed with delight, shucked her blouse over her head to let her skirts fall anywhere they had a mind to, and dropped stark naked to her knees in front of him to whip that towel from his lap.

# Chapter 3

The petite *mestiza* beauty ended her French lesson by getting on top to spit her well-formed tiny torso on the raging shaft of El Brazo Largo, as Longarm was called in Spanish. She described what they had in her by mutual agreement as a *piton grande*, and might have finished on top if Longarm hadn't rolled her on her back to finish right, in full control of the situation with an elbow hooked under either knee to spread her shapely little thighs as wide as they would go.

You had to be there to recall how much a cool drink on a hot day or a hot gal on a cool evening could surprise you by feeling even better than expected. Sometimes, biting into a rare and tender T-bone, a gent who'd only thought he was hungry would suddenly realize he hadn't had a square meal for a spell either. That long train ride from Denver had tingled his balls considerably after that new barmaid at the Black Cat had said no after three teasing walk-homes.

So Consuela got the full benefits of all that frustration, and she seemed to find it flattering. He knew she was going to brag to other Mexican gals about giving her all to the notorious El Brazo Largo. Asking her to be discreet would be like asking a kid stagehand at the Tabor Opera House not to tell his pals he'd spent the night with the prima donna in her dressing room. And he doubted this one would have ripped her duds off quite as free and easy if she hadn't heard others bragging about his famous organ-grinder. He'd no sooner made her come the first time than she shyly confided, "When first I saw all you had for to offer a *muchacha,* was afraid I would never get my jaw for to open so wide! *Pero* now that you have filled my most *furioso* guts with so much . . . *hombre,* I never wish for you to take it out!"

But he had to, before he could shove some more to her dog-style, with his feet on the floor tiles and the part of her blue-black hair pressed to the 'dobe wall on the far side of the bed.

She insisted she'd never had it in that position with a stud horse, or at least a well-hung burro, as they paused to share a cheroot and try for their second winds.

As they cuddled naked, propped up on the pillows with her head on his bare shoulder, Longarm asked if she'd seen one of those horse shows down El Paso way, adding, "No offense, but both your *raza* and mine seem to hit bottom in them stinky little border towns for some reason."

She took a drag, handed the smoke back, and calmly suggested, "Is no mystery. Desperate people who may be wanted on either side of a border are attracted to border towns. *Pero* I am not sure I believe those stories about *putas* who take on a pony or a burro in those, how you say, freak shows?"

Longarm grimaced and said, "It was mighty freaky, even with that canvas sling to keep the burro from getting it all the way in. But to tell the truth, the most freaky part came after, when the master of ceremonies announced that having shown us all she had to offer, the bodacious old lady was offering her gaping maw for four bits more."

He shook his head as if in disbelief of the memory as

22

he told her, "More than one tourist took her up on it. Paid half a dollar to go second to a burro and Lord knows who or what else. I didn't hang around to watch. I'd found her passionate display with the slung-up burro disgusting enough."

Then he took another drag on the cheroot they were sharing, laughed, and confided, "But you know what? There's been times since, alone on the road with just my own fist and imagination for company, when I've sort of wondered what it would have been like with a gal with so much slack betwixt her thighs. She wasn't half bad to look at, and the master of ceremonies said she was able to accommodate all sizes and, in a pinch, unscrew a pickle jar with her amazing ring-dang-doo."

Consuela laughed and said, "You *hombres* all have such dirty minds, and it makes us *mujeres* so happy. Might you have any other tricks you wish for me to perform with a *gatita* I offer for your sole amusement tonight?"

He chuckled fondly, patted her bare shoulder, and nodded at the baggage he'd carried down from Denver with him, draped over the foot of the bed they were sharing, as he confided, "Well, I often carry me some trail rations in them saddlebags. But as luck would have it, I never thought to pack a jar of pickles. Leaving Denver in a hurry, and knowing I'd be stopping off here in the capital first, I just grabbed my old McClellan and Winchester on the fly and figured I'd load up over to the plaza after I hired a mount for my ride to that mining camp."

She said he'd get there way faster if he hopped aboard the narrow-gauge with his possibles. She said she was sure there was more than one livery corral in Gilead if he still felt the need of a *caballo* once he got there.

He repressed a shudder and confided, "There's some things about that particular narrow-gauge line that make me nervous, and I like to sort of ride in unexpected, even when I know the tracks are clear."

23

He took another drag before he asked in a desperately casual tone how she'd heard so much about mad bombers mixing chemicals in a whorehouse toolshed. He observed, "Must be nigh a day's ride from here to Gilead, right?"

She said, "*Sí,* the nearest crests of the Sierra Sangre de Cristo are maybe twenty-five gringo miles to the east. *Pero* Gilead lies in the how-you-say foothills more to the north. If you do not wish for to follow those tracks, you should leave by way of the Bishop's Road, follow the forks that seem to be leading you toward Mount Baldy, and ask directions once you find yourself in another watershed. We know about that *bombadero loco* because we asked. We knew something important to your army was up, so . . ."

"Who told you the War Department was on the prod about Gilead?" he asked with a frown.

She demurely replied, "When one is in the business of running guns down the Rio Bravo and beyond, one concerns oneself with the movements of armies on either side of the border, no? This summer has been good and bad for border jumping. Victorio has been raiding all along this border, and should you run into an *Apache malo* and he sees you first, your border-jumping days may be done. *Pero* on the other hand, if you see *him* first, is not so good for *him,* and thanks to him and all the others riding with Victorio, both your army and *los federales* are too busy for to patrol the border with their usual care."

Longarm insisted, "I know about that Apache scare along the border. We're way north of the border and Gilead is northeast of here! Who told you anyone in the U.S. military was on the prod about Professor MacLennon over to Gilead? Has he sent letters to the President of *Mexico* as well?"

She answered, "Ah, *sí,* I think that was the name they gave us when we asked. We asked some of our people working in Gilead after some of our people working at

Fort Union told us your troops there had been ordered for to stand by on a how-you-say field alert. Our own leaders knew your Ninth and Tenth Cavalries were already in the field after Victorio, with the reserves at Fort Stanton far to the south *not* on standby for to take the field. Then one of our own who works in the the officers' club at Fort Union overheard some troop commanders as they were talking about a forced march here to Santa Fe."

Longarm consulted his mental map, decided an eighty-mile route march around through Glorieta Pass sounded about right, and asked her if she was certain they'd be marching on Santa Fe instead of Gilead itself. "Seems to me if I was out to kill me a spider, I'd head for the center of its web unless I knew for certain which of many a sticky string it might follow to some particular old fly!"

She said she didn't understand.

He said, "Neither do I, unless something new's come up since I left Denver a few hours ago. A self-confessed mad bomber may or may not have the destruction of Downtown Santa Fe in mind. But why wait and see when you know where the threats are coming from? I'm missing something here. Once you point it out, any number of army troopers or local lawmen should have simply gone over to Gilead and picked a letter-writing fool up at his known address!"

Consuela toyed with the hair on Longarm's belly as she casually asked, "*Pero* did you not just say they had sent *you* all the way from Denver, *querido mio*?"

He snuffed the smoke out to take some of her body hair in hand as he answered with a puzzled frown, "They surely did. Have you ever had the feeling there might be something odd about that gingerbread house you'd been invited to with an innocent smile?"

She said she didn't understand that either. So Longarm rolled a delighted Consuela on her back to communicate some more in a manner that called for no explanations.

He'd figured on her staying the night. He'd have liked her to stay the night. But in the wee small hours, after it was quiet downstairs in the cantina, she allowed that her best chance to slip out unseen would be right after everybody else had gone to bed too drunk or too busy to listen sharp.

He didn't argue. He had a lot of thinking to do, thanks to her odd news about his own army, and she'd relaxed his nerves enough to catch a few hours' sleep before he awoke in the morning to the sounds of flowers and the smell of birds.

The morning breeze was scraping a rambling rose vine against his jalousie blinds, and there was a chicken run just below the window.

So he got up and used the corner stand to wash the sleep from his eyes and Consuela from his crotch before he got dressed. He decided to spring for the shave he could use at a local barbershop. A stranger in town could hear a lot in a barbershop without appearing too nosy.

He knew Lemonade Lucy would say he was on duty that morning. But she was in Washington, D.C., and nobody from the Denver office was likely to tell on him. So he got out a sailcloth work shirt and a pair of clean but faded jeans, and replaced them in his saddlebag with the rolled-up tobacco tweed that tended to cramp his style.

Looking and feeling more cow, Longarm put his tweed vest on over the work shirt, seeing it was a tad crisp outside to begin with and vest pockets were handy for notebooks, three-for-a-nickel cheroots, and a gold-washed chain with a pocket watch at one end and a pocket derringer at the other.

Standing tall before the pier glass in his low-heeled stovepipe boots, Longarm squared his pancaked Stetson cavalry-style and buckled his gun rig to pack his six-gun butt-first on his left hip, offering a slightly faster cross draw

26

than a man could expect from under a pesky frock coat.

Then he stuck a fresh cheroot between his teeth and, locking things up, dropped to one knee in the dark hall to wedge a match stem under the bottom hinge of the door.

When he met up with a chambermaid on the stairs, he ticked his hat brim to her, tipped her a dime, and told her he didn't want her in his hired quarters for cleaning. She smilingly allowed it was no skin off her brown ass if he liked his bedding messy.

He didn't. But he could tidy up after himself if he had to, and it was more important to know nobody had been going through his possibles and papers while he was out. There was something funny about this case. Until he knew more about it, he'd set his usually more trusting attitude aside with those itchy tweed pants.

Out front, the lemon sunlight of a New Mexico springtime dazzled the eye without really heating things up worth mentioning. Longarm could have eaten at the *posada*. But he chose to breakfast at a stand-up chili joint along the *calle* from the railroad yards to the central plaza. He'd eaten there before and knew they made chil con carne right. More importantly, he wanted to get the feel of the streets of Santa Fe, as they might or might not have changed since his last visit a spell back.

As he stood at the counter, washing down his chili and tortillas with black coffee or paint remover—it was hard to tell when Mexican chili slingers started out to make coffee—Longarm was able to watch passersby in the mirror over the grill.

He didn't see any army uniforms. That didn't mean there were none in town, of course. But there didn't seem to be more troopers than usual from a garrison a hard two days' ride away. You usually saw more officers and noncoms in the big city on weekends, unless they came in on government business. The town of Las Vegas, much closer to Fort Union and big enough for a soldier on leave with thirteen

27

dollars burning a hole in his pocket on payday, drew most of the army action in northern New Mexico.

Despite its current official ownership, Santa Fe was still more a Mexican Anglo community, with enough assimilated Indians to keep the two Christian communities on fairly friendly terms. Few of Santa Fe's Acama, Hopi, Laguna, Navajo, or Zuni visitors rode in looking for trouble. Most had something to sell. Some were there for coin silver or turquoise from the nearby Cerillos mines. Longarm had never heard of an Indian trading for bat shit.

Only a few in the morning crowd seemed Anglo. Cowhands didn't get into town much on working days. So that was why Longarm noticed the rider wearing shotgun chaps and a Schofield .45 Short when his face appeared twice in the mirror within less than five minutes.

The third time he started past, the strange rider stopped, facing Longarm's back, and looked both ways, more than once, before his gun hand dropped to the grips of that Schofield, even as their eyes met in the mirror.

The stranger intent on shooting Longarm in the back, seeing he was in for it now, like it or not, drew as his very life depended on it.

For it did, just as Longarm's life depended on beating the son of a bitch to the draw!

Whirling off his stool, Longarm threw that mug of black coffee in his free hand as he went for his own gun with the other in the slow, dreamy process of dropping to the walk on his right side and shoulder as they both fired.

Then, seeing he still seemed able, Longarm fired again, then again in a space of less than two full seconds, as he sprawled on the walk in a confusion of earsplitting gunshots and eye-blinding gun smoke while he tried to figure out what in blue blazes he was doing, even as he just kept doing it.

# Chapter 4

Like most experienced gun hands, Longarm had only packed five in the wheel lest he shoot a fool toe off. So he had to stop firing his .44-40 and draw his double derringer after he'd fired a fifth round blind into swirling white confusion. This gave the gun smoke time to lift from the brick walk so Longarm could see a still-smoking Schofield all alone on the bricks. He held his fire until, sure enough, he could make out the man who'd drawn that Schofield a few yards out in the dusty dirt *calle*. He lay on his back smiling up at the sky with his knees drawn up and thighs spread wide as a whore's on payday. Since the leather chaps on his thighs didn't cover the crotch of his own jeans, there was quite a puddle of piss wetting down the dust under and all about his dead ass.

Longarm was back on his feet and still reloading when an older man with a pewter star pinned to his own vest joined him near the body, a thoughtful hand on his own gun grips, as he quietly introduced himself as the Santa Fe County law, anxiously awaiting some answers as to why there seemed to be a dead body in his jurisdiction.

Longarm said, "I'm law too. Federal. I feel certain that gent on the far side of yon counter will agree this total-ass stranger drew on me just now from behind. I have no idea why."

The county deputy shot a questioning look at the Mexican who ran the chili joint. Longarm decided to leave a handsome tip when the swarthy gray cuss nodded and called out, "*Es verdad*. The *vaquero gringo* drew first. I still do not see how this customer of mine could have won. I ducked under this counter when the shooting started!"

The older local lawman smiled thinly at Longarm and said, "There you go. I've known Hernan there long enough to doubt he'd lie to me without good reason. Would you care to show me some identification so's I can be sure you ain't married to his sister?"

Longarm put both his six-gun and derringer away to break out his wallet and flash his badge and deputy marshal's warrant. By this time they'd been joined by another county man and a uniformed roundsman from the Santa Fe police. So the first lawman on the scene called out, "It's all right, gents. The one who won's with us. He's that federal man from Denver they told us about. The one called Longarm. It seems this cadaver in the shotgun chaps took exception to his visit and drew on him just now."

A younger county lawman who read the *Police Gazette* from time to time shot a bemused look down at the dead man and decided, "He must have busted up with his true love and wanted to end it all. I reckon I'd just suck on my barrel and pull the trigger if I was that intent on ending it all. They say some of the gents who've slapped leather on this old boy have spent a painful few minutes dying!"

The uniformed copper badge dryly remarked, "This one never knew what hit him. You can tell by the way he's pissed his pants. I think I've seen the pissy rascal over by the plaza, pestering Mex gals just last night during El Paseo. I tried to tell him he was going about El Paseo

30

wrong. He told me to mind my own beeswax. I figured it was only a question of time before somebody cleaned his plow for him. A disrespectful mouth, a Schofield .45, and a tendency to draw on grown men with serious reps is not the recipe *my* mamma gave us for a long and healthy existence!"

The senior county lawman suggested a search of the body. So one of the younger deputies dropped to one knee to gingerly go through the dead man's pockets.

When he found a battered wallet containing eight paper dollars and a Denver library card made out to one Samuel Adams, the deputy proved he had some experience by declaring, "Heaps of owlhoot riders take out library cards or even a voter's registration just by asking, under as original a name as John Smith or Samuel Adams, for Gawd's sake!"

They found a more serious twenty-dollar gold piece and some silver cartwheels in another pocket, along with a snotty kerchief and some sheep-gut condoms in a package that had been opened.

The copper badge shrugged and decided, "So he got lucky at El Paseo with some *puta* no more interested in delicacy. The question before the house is why on earth he followed Longarm here down from Denver!"

Longarm shook his head and said, "I follow your drift about library cards, pard. But he never followed me to Santa Fe. I just got in last night. If he'd known I was in town or expected me in town, he wouldn't have been at any Paseo with his bare face hanging out. So he was here ahead of me and *not* expecting me, until he spotted me and got all hot and bothered about it just now!"

By this time a considerable crowd was gathering, along with more copper badges, one of them wearing a sergeant's stripes. So Longarm had to tell his tale all over, and it was commencing to get tedious when he suggested it might be best to get the dead man over to the morgue and tell the county coroner he was dead.

The police sergeant said he'd already thought of that, and as he took charge, Longarm took that first county man aside to quietly ask who'd told them he'd be coming down from Denver.

The county lawman didn't sound evasive as he calmly replied, "The military police. They've asked us to ban soldiers blue from the plaza and surrounding cantinas and saloons. Seems some sore loser from the Lost Cause has been threatening to blow up every such soldier west of the Big Muddy. They say they have no idea why. They just want to make it tougher to blow soldiers blue apart until they can figure out some way to prevent it!"

Longarm scowled down at the dead man at their feet as he muttered, "Nobody around here figures to offer any good suggestions. I'm missing something here. I got to get over to the Hall of Records and take me some notes. I'll be there or at the Posada con Vista Linda if anybody needs me. Could you clear that with the coroner's office and Santa Fe police, Sheriff?"

The older lawman said, "Undersheriff. Undersheriff Taylor, Hiram Taylor, at your service, Longarm. Like we told the provost marshal's shavetail, sheriff's office calls the tune in these parts. Calling for anyone else can be a waste of breath since we got the new Governor from Washington. Old Lew tidied up after the Ring by confirming some few of us in office, firing way more, and kicking the ones he wasn't able to fire up the stairs. That's political science, you understand. When a political appointee can't be fired or put in jail, you promote him out of reach of the cookie jar. Most of the gents in office as sheriffs or county supervisors in New Mexico right now are honest enough for the new Governor. Local police are honest enough for their townships, I reckon, but of course they don't have any police powers outside their townships, if you see what I mean."

Longarm saw what he meant. One of the things about the wide-open spaces west of, say, Longitude 100° was how wide-open spaces could *get* out this way. Eastern counties were usually no more than thirty or forty miles across, divided into six-by-six-mile townships, whether there was a town in each or not. So back East, no county resident had more than twenty miles to travel to the county courthouse, while the three miles at most to the local justice of the peace could be managed in an hour *on foot*. But Western counties could be four or five times a sensible size, with the county line two or more days in the saddle for a posse, while a town marshal could chase a serious offender three miles at most.

Longarm cautiously told Undersheriff Taylor, "You've made mention of your new Governor. You've made mention of the military police and the two brands of local civilian lawmen on tap. Don't you have even one U.S. marshal, like my own boss, Billy Vail, here in the New Mexico Territory?"

The county lawman snorted, "Hell, sure we do. More than one. They appoint a marshal to go with each federal district court, don't they?"

Longarm said, "They're sure supposed to. So how come I was invited to this party, and where are all the *other* kids?"

Taylor looked more confused. Longarm insisted, "I ride for another court up Colorado way. If the federally appointed Governor of New Mexico Territory has been threatened by a mad bomber or, hell, a lovesick chambermaid, how come your deputy marshals riding for federal districts here in New Mexico Territory ain't willing, able, and anxious to do something about it?"

"They're busy, I reckon," the older lawman answered easily, adding, "Nobody can blow Governor Lew Wallace up here in Santa Fe right now. He's down in Las Cruces or maybe Mesilla. Cleaning up some more shit left over from the Ring. I understand he took some federal deputies along with his guard detachment, because of those threats against his life. Does anybody have to tell you why the military down that way might want to saddle others with some chores?"

Longarm grimaced and said, "Victorio's been making the front pages of the *Rocky Mountain News*. But like that old church song advises, farther along we'll know more about it. So I'll bring you up to date on what I find out today later at the coroner's hearing."

They shook on it and parted friendly.

It was a short walk in low heels to the central plaza with most new government facilities occupying the same 'dobe buildings as the old pre-war administrations, first from Spain and later from Mexico City. Adobe was just gumbo mud mixed with cow shit and straw to give it a little character. But when you built thick walls with it right, and the old Pueblo Indian masons had built around that plaza right, they lasted forever in a halfway dry climate.

A heap of *ramada-* or veranda-fronted church properties, and even some of the original Governor's Palace, had been put to more utilitarian use by Anglo-Americanos. So when Longarm saw he was passing a substation of the army provost marshal, he decided to stop there first.

The sergeant major presiding from behind a sort of judge's bench only had to hear a little before he summoned a corporal to lead their civilian fellow lawman back to see the adjutant.

This turned out to be a first lieutenant named Lowell, and Longarm liked him, even if he did have a Boston accent. Lieutenant Lowell sat him down and offered him a cigar with a sort of sneaky smile. Once the two of them were lit up, Lowell confirmed that Santa Fe was indeed

34

barred to troops on leave from Fort Union until further notice. When Longarm asked how come, Lowell answered easily, "They told us you'd been filled in about that former Confederate chemist over in the Sangre de Cristos, Deputy Long. Governor Wallace is out of town, but he's made vile threats against the military as well."

"So how come nobody has seen fit to just ride over to Gilead and bring the silly bastard in dead or alive?" Longarm asked.

The military police officer beamed and said, "The colonel said you'd say something like that. Is it true they call you Longarm, and are you really the one who knocked Provost Marshal Walthers on his ass twice?"

Longarm shrugged modestly and quietly explained, "I had to. He kept bitching about the *first* time I had to knock him on his ass. It was nothing personal. He just kept getting in my way."

Lieutenant Lowell grinned like a mean little kid and said, "Remind me not to ever get in your way. We *have* sent riders over to Gilead to see about Professor Mac-Lennon. More than one. More than once. We were told the U.S. marshal's office here in Santa Fe tried to serve him with a warrant, to no avail."

"I was wondering why they'd handed *me* the shovel," Longarm grumbled, asking, "What happened? Couldn't they locate him, or did somebody bulge a muscle at 'em?"

Lowell soberly replied, "Both. He doesn't seem to be staying at that house of ill repute we were told about. Madam Claudette was gracious about showing our riders around, and offered to suck them off free. Nobody else they interviewed seemed to know anything about Professor MacLennon. They worked so hard at not knowing anything about him that they gave the impression they were scared skinny of the obvious lunatic."

"You say that scared your riders off?" Longarm asked with an eyebrow raised.

The first lieutenant shook his head and turned in his swivel chair to open a file drawer as he replied, "Not exactly. The civilian lawmen who rode over to Gilead got the impression they were flailing around in a fog as well. Someone had to know something, but nobody seemed to know anything. And then we got this letter, postmarked Gilead. Where else?"

He handed it across to Longarm, who for the first time saw what a childish scrawl their self-proclaimed mad bomber really wrote with. It wasn't clear whether MacLennon was accusing the military police of solemnity or sodomy, but he'd made some effort to write clearly when he warned, "None of you can hope to thwart me because nobody in all of Gilead knows just where I've placed my little beauties. Suffice it to say they've been fitted with very delicate detonators, fashioned from test tubes of $H_2SO_4$ poised very very delicately. So walk softly when you walk by me, you Damnyankee Slavefuckers, and ask my faithful Jeremiah if you doubt me! Jeremiah will tell you that's right!"

Longarm handed the letter back, murmuring, "Sulfuric acid ought to do it. They warn high school chemists to be careful about pouring $H_2SO_4$ in warm water! It's that Jeremiah bullshit I can't get a handle on."

The army man suggested, "Wasn't Professor Mac-Lennon a slaveholder before the war and weren't slaves often given names from the Good Book?"

Longarm shrugged, allowed Jeremiah was less silly than Caesar or Aristotle, and explained, "In other such notes he seemed to think this mysterious Jeremiah was another chemist, a church here in New Mexico, or a street in Charleston. This lady I spoke to from Charleston says there's no such street there. Nobody at the University of Virginia can recall any member of the faculty named Jeremiah."

"There's no Church of Jeremiah in Santa Fe," the officer said. "If I recall my own Sunday school days correctly, the Prophet Jeremiah from the Old Testament does not appear in the New Testament, where most of the Anglican, Catholic, and Lutheran saints first appear."

Longarm took a thoughtful drag on the fine cigar, flicked ash in a hospitable glass tray on his side of the desk, and decided, "I suspect the professor's really pissed off at some Jeremiah he hates so hard he keeps misplacing him. I'm commencing to see why some slick rascal up and asked for me by name. Through no intent of my own I seem to have a rep for delicate chores, and he says them tubes of acid are poised delicately over his nitroglycerine."

He heaved a weary sigh and added, "What sort of contingent plans has the army made if I walk into a booby trap in Gilead and get blown to itty-bitty pieces?"

The army man replied without a trace of shame, "Oh, in that case we mean to just surround Gilead with field artillery and blow everything and everybody to itty-bitty pieces. They figure if you can't do it a nicer way, it can't be done any nicer way. So what the hell?"

# Chapter 5

First lieutenants had been known to make mistakes, and it wasn't far out of his way. So Longarm ambled across the plaza to the handy old Spanish church, flashed his badge at an altar boy, and wound up sharing some sangria with a likeable balding priest called Padre Fernando in the rectory next door. You could tell by the bookshelves all around that Padre Fernando liked to read, in English and French, as well as the Spanish you'd expect.

As they sat by the cold fireplace, sipping fruit punch without much punch, the local priest not only allowed there was no Church of Jeremiah in Santa Fe, but that he'd recently read both volumes of *Ben Hur*.

"I was curious when I heard our new Governor was an author," Padre Fernando confided, in the tone of a man defending his poker losses. So Longarm explained how Professor Norman MacLennon had accused Lew Wallace of insulting Saint Thomas and advised him to check on this at the Church of Jeremiah.

Padre Fernando pursed his thin lips and closed his eyes in thought before he decided, "I recall no mention of any Christian saint in *Ben Hur*. Was more a rousing adventure story than a religious novel, and I confess I enjoyed it and found nothing objectionable in it, despite it being written by a Protestant."

"Nothing about Saint Thomas?" Longarm insisted.

The priest shook his head and said, "Very little about the Passion of Our Lord at all, as a matter of fact. *Ben Hur* is the saga of a young Hebrew aristocrat stripped of his wealth and enslaved by the Romans for a crime he did not commit."

"I read the book, Padre," Longarm told him politely.

Padre Fernando nodded and replied, "In that case you will recall it takes Ben Hur the better part of two volumes to regain his freedom, make a new fortune, and return to the Holy Land to find his old family estate in some disrepair with his mother and younger sister outcasts, forced to live with other lepers."

"In a cave." Longarm nodded. "They surely were in a fix. But then Jesus passes by and cures all the lepers, so . . . Right, it's only in the last chapter that Mr. Ben Hur makes up his mind to follow the new faith. Neither Jesus himself nor any of his disciples appear in the book on stage, as they say at the opera house. So tell me something, Padre. Do you suppose a sore loser brooding about some Thomas Jeremiah or a Jeremiah Thompson could get his real enemy mixed up with a book an imaginary enemy just published to some acclaim?"

The priest looked confused until Longarm explained what he'd read about lunatics replacing unbearable hatreds with hatreds they were able to handle better with their twisted brains.

The priest smiled thinly and murmured, "One hears some impossible tales of woe in the confessional. Is possible this Jeremiah Thompson was not the one who sinned, but one a very disturbed man may have *wronged* in the past and, as you put it, *brooded* about. But who could we be talking about either way?"

Longarm said, "I don't know. I mean to wire my office

and let them see if they can find out. There must be lists of chemists he could have stolen formula off of, or vice versa. His Jeremiah or his Thomas could be some Confederate official he had words with. It could even be some student who played a practical joke on him in the chemistry lab. Chemistry students are forever causing stinks or explosions and some professors have no sense of humor."

The priest said, "My word, you do have some long lists to go over!"

To which Longarm cheerfully replied, "Not *me,* Padre. We got us a file clerk paid to handle chores like that. I only need a little more from the local Hall of Records before I can saddle up and ride over to the Sangre de Cristos."

As they both rose, Padre Fernando soberly asked, "Do you feel that is wise, my son? They say the maniac has hidden bombs all in and around Gilead! There seems no argument that he is a madman, driven by some twisted hatred of authority!"

Longarm didn't ask who might have told their own Mexican priest about that. He confided, "I wasn't figuring on riding in with my badge on my vest, Padre. Gilead's a mining camp of three or four hundred souls who must still go to and from work, buy butter and eggs, at least, off the usual surrounding produce farms, and ride in or out of town in quest of it all. I ain't wearing my usual suit, and I can just as easily hire a Mexican saddle to replace my usual McClellan when I go to the livery and hire a mount. Ain't no way our mad bomber can have an eye on every which way into town, and even if he sees another good old boy riding in off the range, who's to say he don't belong there?"

The priest said firmly, "Almost anyone who *does* belong in Gilead, of course. The *pobercito* from Gilead who told *us* about the situation over there says the *bombadero loco* and his friends are holding half the town hostage,

41

threatening to blow the whole place up if anyone there refuses to do as they are told!"

"What have they been told to do?" asked Longarm with interest.

The priest explained, "Many of the lesser lights of Gilead have been able for to slip away, of course. Those more important to the running of a railhead settlement have been ordered for to go on about business as usual and, of course, report anything unusual to the piano player at a certain house of ill repute."

Longarm nodded and said, "Madam Claudette's place. Pretty cagey. A whorehouse hardcase who ain't a known member of their gang reporting to the gang on any strangers riding in. Them other lawmen were under the gun all the time they were in town, but the professor held his fire and let them leave alive when he saw they weren't even warm. So that might offer another way to skin the cat. Do you know that old church song 'Farther Along,' Padre?"

The priest smiled thinly and replied, "I believe that is a Protestant hymn, my son."

Longarm allowed it still made sense, no offense, but refrained from humming it before he was back out front and crossing to the Hall of Records on the same side of the plaza as the Governor's Palace.

Inside, the sudden cool shade reminded him how sunny and warm it was getting outside this late in the morning. The mousy gal wearing glasses and a pencil in the bun of her brown hair came over to the counter to confirm that he was right about that noonday sun out on the plaza. She said, "I'm sorry, sir. We're about to close for the next four hours. We follow the local custom of *la siesta* here in Santa Fe. I know it's a bother, but what can we do when two thirds or more of the population knocks off until four?"

Then she took a closer look, squinting through her thick

glasses in the dim light, and gasped, "Custis Long! Is that really you, you mean old thing?"

To which he could only reply, "I plead guilty to that, Miss Tess. Albeit I don't recall treating anybody hereabouts with anything but all due respect last time I was in town."

Then he asked, "Weren't you working as a stenographer gal for that other Governor, ma'am?"

She stepped around the counter and moved over to the doorway as she said, "You know I was, and it was kind of you to put in a good word for me about that Indian beef contract. Governor Wallace says he knows I was only trying to do the job they were paying me for. So he gave me this job instead of firing me."

She shut and locked the oak door he'd come through. "There, that's better," she added. "Nobody will bother us before four, and what can I do for you, Custis?"

He doubted she meant that the way it could be taken. Lots of big-eyed gals with myopia stared out at their worlds in a sort of sultry way without meaning to.

He gulped and said, "I'm down here some more on government beeswax, Miss Tess. Before I ride over to Gilead, I'd like to go through your files for mining claims, property deeds, business charters, and stuff like so."

She said, "Oh, pooh, you're after that mad bomber and this time your excuse will be that you've been blown to bits!"

"I didn't know I'd done anything as called for excusing, ma'am," he replied with a puzzled frown.

She said, "Oh, come on, you know I'd have never let you see those private papers of the previous territorial administration if you hadn't gotten round me with your sweet talk and bedroom eyes. You knew I'd heard all about you from other federal working girls and I felt so . . . *left out* when you just arrested those Indian Agency gents and left for Denver without even saying good-bye!"

43

He thought back and decided, "Well, sure I said good-bye, just up the way at the federal courthouse, Miss Tess. You'd turned state's evidence, and I even walked you home afterward. You live a furlong or so to the northwest, over by that feeder of the Rio Grande they call the Santa Fe as well."

"And you shook my hand and turned away when you got me to my door!" she almost wailed, moving a step nearer, which seemed near indeed when you were alone with even a mousy gal behind a locked door.

He smiled down at her uncertainly and asked, "Well, what was a man supposed to do, once he'd walked a witness home from a hearing? Ask himself in for the night?"

She smiled up adoringly and confessed, "I was hoping so hard that you would, Custis. As you may have noticed, I'm rather shy by nature and I seldom walk anywhere with a man as . . . popular with the girls as you seem to be."

Longarm sighed and said, "I really did come to look through your files, then and now, but I know how hard it is to concentrate on federal business when you have monkey business in mind. So just let me know when you want me to stop, if a little slap-and-tickle might make it easier to work with you."

He took her in his arms and kissed her, hard and French, expecting that to inspire second thoughts. A lot of flirty gals seemed to have second thoughts once a man took them up on their flutterings.

But Tess Bronson tongued him back and groped for the buttons of his fly as she did so. He didn't want her busting any buttons down yonder. So he reached down to whip his old organ-grinder out and just hand it over, already rising to the occasion.

She hung on tight and led him by the pecker like a big old pull toy until she had him on his back across her counter, which was so high his heels were off the floor

44

and she hardly had to bend at all to go down on him as she proceeded to undress her shy self.

So they both wound up stark naked atop the counter, with him on top and her high buttons crossed around the nape of Longarm's neck to spare her tailbone from the firm blotter under her rollicking rump as she rolled her head from side to side and moaned about princes who came at last.

She was much prettier without her glasses, but thanks to Consuela at the *posada,* bless her tawny hide, Longarm took longer than most men would have to come in the even more passionate Anglo gal.

She took this as a compliment, or maybe an opportunity that a gal so shy seldom had. When she did come, ahead of him, she was strumming her own banjo like a young gal who jerked off more often than she enjoyed the real thing. But when he really got to moving in her a second time, she let go of her clit and just rubbed her belly against his, moaning, "Oh, Dear Lord, this is the way I really like it!"

That made two of them. So a fine time was had by all until, as they were going at it dog-style with her gripping the seat of the chair she usually rested her sweet ass on, Longarm heard what could have been distant thunder. So he said, "Might be a good notion to get dressed again, Miss Tess. If that's a summer rain squall coming, some of your Anglo customers may come pounding on yonder door before you open at four."

She arched her spine and begged for more.

He gave her more. But the next time she came, he got her to agree they'd be more comfortable, and less out of breath, if they saved a few strokes for after supper at her place by the river.

But nobody bothered them as Longarm spent the better part of two hours taking notes from the extensive files.

Considering how recently Uncle Sam had taken New

Mexico away from Old Mexico, they sure had accumulated a mess of paperwork, from voter registrations to old Spanish land grants honored by the new government under the terms of that peace treaty with Mexico back in '48. He saw the original Mexican owners of all that bat shit had sold out to a seed and farm supply syndicate with offices back East but a mineral claim filed out New Mexico way. They were chartered to just refine crude bat shit to industrial-grade fertilizer and ship it by rail in bulk. There was nothing saying how you refined bat shit.

There were two slaughterhouses in Gilead. Both sold a little beef locally, but made most of their money on hides and tallow Spanish-style. So there was one tannery and one rendering plant, serving all comers. All four firms dealing with purely local range stock were owned by long-established New Mexican Mexican families, without a former Confederate in the bunch.

That wasn't surprising. New Mexico Territory had been plagued by rebel raiders during the war, but remained with the Union. Even if it hadn't, none of the bigger Texas outfits moving into the Pecos Valley of late would be interested in peddling hides and tallow on a modest scale in Gilead.

To begin with, Gilead was on the western slope of the Sangre de Cristos, which formed a watershed between the upper Rio Grande and the parallel south-flowing Pecos. The tricky rail connections between Santa Fe and markets to the northeast kept it from becoming an important cattle town. Big outfits down along the Pecos, such as the Jingle Bob and the Maxwell Grant, drove their market herds up the far side of the Sangre de Cristos along the Goodnight-Loving Trail to Colorado or beyond. Longarm decided it was more likely Professor MacLennon and his mysterious pals had simply commandeered a remote, mostly Mexican mining camp at the handy spur-head of a mountain narrow-gauge with the intent to do . . . what?

As he explained to Tess Bronson while she pinned her hair up some more, "Raving lunatics generally work alone. It's hard to recruit a faithful band of followers when *they* take you for teched in the head."

She demurely asked why MacLennon's mysterious followers couldn't be sort of strange themselves.

He shook his head and insisted, "We're missing something about all these death threats. Nobody's been killed as yet, and some Mexicans I know think the professor's in with regular outlaws. A famous bank robber, she called one of 'em."

*"She?"* purred the Anglo gal he'd been humping.

Longarm said, "I told you I'd take you to supper and carry you on home later. Right now I have to go ask at the sheriff's department about famous bank robbers in these parts!"

And so that was Longarm's intent once he'd kissed Tess good-bye and headed over to the handy sheriff's office. But before he got as far as the door, it flew open and Undersheriff Taylor popped out like a cuckoo clock bird to exclaim, "Where have you been! We've been looking all over town for you!"

Longarm said, "Well, you've found me. So never mind where I might have been. What's up? Are they holding that coroner's inquest earlier than I expected?"

The older lawman heaved a sigh of relief and declared, "For a few minutes there we expected you'd be the *subject* of an inquest. But lucky for you, you weren't enjoying the siesta at your *posada* when a person or persons unknown kicked in your door and emptied a double-barrel ten-gauge into your hired bed this afternoon!"

# Chapter 6

They'd moved his McClellan and possibles to their own stable's tack room, and better yet, had a remuda of mounts he was welcome to pick from. But seeing there was still time, Longarm went back to the *posada* to settle up and look the scene over.

They'd about cleaned up the mess when he arrived. A double load of 00 buck didn't make that much of a mess of a bed when there was nobody in it. The *posadero*, Tio Paco, allowed Longarm was *muy sangre azul,* or a real gent, when he insisted on paying for the shot-up bedding, with drinks all around for the scare.

Nobody scared had laid eyes on the rascal or rascals making all the noise upstairs, of course. Gents who worked or drank in cantinas were smart enough to just hit the floor and stay there until the smoke cleared whenever they heard guns going off.

As he'd hoped, Longarm was able to get little Consuela to one side. Nobody close enough to listen in spoke enough English to matter as she suggested a position they hadn't tried yet for later.

He confided, "I've found another place to hide out tonight, seeing somebody here in town seems so cross with me. But it looks as if I may need to call on you and your rebel friends for help after all."

Consuela beamed and replied without hesitation, "Your wish is our command. Name it and I shall see your commands are carried out to the very letter and then, later, when I have you alone in that hideout . . ."

"I don't want you hiding out with me where I'll be hiding out," he told her. "It might not be safe for you there. I know I'll feel safer knowing you're out of the . . . line of fire. What I really want from you and your rebel pals might be dangerous enough to ask."

She dared him to name it.

He explained his suspicion that any strangers riding into Gilead were likely to be reported to the piano player in that house of ill repute. He said, "I need to sort of drift in and hide in plain sight amid gents known to belong in town. They'll expect a stranger to be scouting for a place to saddle his pony, stuff his face, and rest his weary head in the wee small hours. If I was to quarter and hang out with some of your own kind over yonder . . ."

"*Pero* you are *Anglo*!" she objected with an uncertain smile.

Longarm said, "I can ride a *vaquero* saddle as easily as I can ride my old army rig. I've got a good tan, and you have to get close to me to see the color of my eyes under this hat brim. Being took for your kind or mine is largely a question of *expectation*. Most folks take Pete Maxwell, down to Fort Summer, as a big Anglo cattle baron, on account he runs a lot of cows on a lot of range and sometimes forgets to tell folks his Mexican momma named him Pedro."

She cocked a brow up at him and decided, "Perhaps if we got you a straw sombrero and some *charro* pants for to wear . . ."

Longarm shook his head and said, "Not hardly. Few if any New Mexico riders of any ancestry gussy up like border *buscaderos*. My plan will only work if nobody on the other side looks *close* at me. If anybody in Gilead takes enough interest in me to worry about my pants, they ain't likely to buy this child as a poor but honest *vaquero charro*."

She told him he was *loco en la cabeza*, but offered to guide him on over and introduce him around in back to some other followers of La Causa Mejico Libre. There were too many others in view to kiss on it, so they shook on it, and he agreed it might be best to get a predawn start and drift into Gilead with some farm produce in the morning.

As he was fixing to go, she asked if they were likely to encounter the followers of that *ladrone muy malo* General Sí Sí on the trail.

When she confirmed that this General Sí Sí was the notorious bank robber she'd mentioned before, Longarm confessed, "General Sí Sí is a new one on me. I've never heard of him. You say he's famous for robbing banks in these parts?"

She answered simply, "*Sí*. I was little at the time *pero* I remember how excited everyone became when General Sí Sí and his *banditos* robbed all the banks in Santa Fe on the same day! Was a very big gang General Sí Sí had, and they stole many *caballos* as well!"

Longarm suddenly laughed like hell and asked, "Hold on, you must mean General Sibley, C.S.A., raiding up out of Texas during the war!"

She nodded and replied, "*Sí*, I think that sounds more like his Anglo name. As I said, I was very little at the time!"

"You surely grew up nice," Longarm responded gallantly. Then he said, "Hold on. Brigadier H. H. Sibley, C.S.A., was a Confederate Army officer. Sort of. I was fighting back East where both sides had real soldiers in the field. But I understand things were less formal out in these parts."

He thought back to what he'd read about a campaign he hadn't been invited to partake of, and decided, "You must be talking about that time General Sibley occupied Santa Fe for a few days. He did ride off with everything that wasn't nailed down, once Union Regulars and the Colorado Militia convinced him he wasn't going to seize the Colorado goldfields up around Pikes Peak after all. But that all happened a good spell back in the middle of a war. You're not trying to tell us General H. H. Sibley and his Confederate raiders have come back for a second go-round with the U.S. Army, are you?"

Consuela shrugged her tawny bare shoulders and answered simply, "Is what some say. If not General Sí Sí himself, perhaps some of the *ladrones* in gray who rode up here with him the last time. The *soldados azul* are most busy with *indios malos* this spring. The older ones say the last time your army was busy in the East, *los indios malos* were able to raid at will in the West. Perhaps these other *soldados* they beat that time think they might do better when the *soldados azul* are busy with Victorio, no?"

Longarm allowed he sure hoped she was wrong and, on that cheerful note, headed back to the plaza and managed a quick late lunch before he had to attend that inquest on the stranger he'd shot that morning.

He wasn't as strange by that evening. Both the sheriff's department and Santa Fe police had been asking around. A copper badge had come up with a barkeep who'd heard the dead man and a shorter towheaded pal talking about some action they'd see once they contacted some pal they called the Old Sarge. A deputy sheriff had traced those shotgun chaps to a local Mexican leather worker after the barkeep failed to recall either stranger in such serious range gear. If that Denver library card meant anything, the man who'd been packing it along with a Schofield

52

army-surplus .45-Short had been riding more open range before arriving in serious chaparral country. The Mexican who'd sold him the chaps recalled his name as "Call-me-Sam Adams." They were still working on a name for the shorter towheaded one. The barkeep wasn't sure, but he thought the dead one might have called him Red, or Reb. Reb made more sense if a man had almost-white blond hair.

The hearing was held in an unused chamber of what had been a mission school in Spanish times. So it smelled like they were underground as soon as the unventilated space got stuffy. It got stuffy because so many gents, from the rival local newspaper reporters to that adjutant from the provost marshal's, Lieutenant Lowell, seemed interested in such a mysterious shoot-out.

When asked, Longarm opined it worked more than one way for him. He said, "Call-me-Sam could have assumed I'd followed him down from Denver and decided he'd best slap leather first. I've wired my home office a progress report. If there's a recent federal warrant out on any pair as fits such a description, they'll doubtless wire that back. On the other hand, if at least one of 'em answers to Reb, that might tie in with other rumors I've been hearing about trouble brewing in these parts. I feel sure a heap of you New Mexico riders will recall the depredations of General H. H. Sibley, C.S.A., during that misunderstanding betwixt the states."

Lieutenant Lowell objected. "Just a moment, Longarm. Didn't General H. H. Sibley ride for the Union?"

Longarm soberly replied, "He did if you're talking about one Major General Henry Hastings Sibley. *Brigadier* General Henry *Hopkin* Sibley rode for the Confederacy. West Texas Militia, to be specific. History can sure get confusing."

He let that sink in and proceeded. "The H. H. Sibley out of Texas came tearing up the Rio Grande, took this town of Santa Fe from its light Union garrison, and robbed everybody blind for as long as it lasted."

He added, "I'm sorry, Lieutenant. Facts is facts, and the regulars were too busy with Lee's Army of Virginia to hold Santa Fe against a way bigger bunch. Old Sibley bragged he aimed to march on up to Pikes Peak or beyond and seize the Colorado goldfields for the South. But as most of you know, the Colorado Militia never waited for him to come to them. They marched south lickety-split, and met up with Sibley's columns over to the Sangre de Cristos, where Chivington chopped up their advance guard at Pigeon Ranch, wiped out their supply train at Apache Canyon, and led the charge at Glorieta Pass, the crazy son of a bitch."

A newpaper man waved a pencil to demand, "Back up and run that item about Chivington past me again, Deputy Long. Are you talking about that same Colonel John Chivington who disgraced himself and the Third Colorado at the Massacre of Sand Creek?"

Longarm nodded and soberly replied, "You just heard me say history can get confusing and you heard me call him a crazy son of a bitch. He was a major under a Colonel Slough nobody recalls, for the same reasons nobody remembers Terry was in command of the bunch Custer was scouting for at Little Big Horn. John Chivington was a physical giant they'd forgot to install any physical fear in. He was a Methodist minister when he wasn't on active duty with the Colorado Militia. He was in the van of Slough's column, all the way down from Denver, and when he rid into a rebel ambush at the Pigeon Ranch along the Santa Fe trail through the south end of the Sangre de Cristos, the rebels out to ambush him were in a whole lot of trouble."

Someone in the dark smoke-filled room muttered, "I heard Chivington was a murderous butcher!"

Longarm said, "He was. He butchered lots of old boys

at Pigeon Ranch and tortured prisoners, some say, to find out where their supply train was at the moment. Then he led a wild-ass charge down the wall of Apache Canyon and butchered Sibley's supply train, loaded up with loot from hereabouts. Colonel Slough and the main Colorado column dug in at Glorieta Pass gave the Texans pause. Then Chivington charged and got them all running, clean down the Rio Grande and out of the war. Like Custer, Chivington should have quit whilst he was ahead. But a short time later, as we all know, he led his part-time troopers off the Paths of Glory down that Road to Hell that's paved with good intentions."

"You mean Sand Creek?" the same reporter asked.

Longarm nodded and said, "Old Chivington's intentions were swell. They'd promoted him and put him in command of his own regiment after he'd saved Colorado and helped take New Mexico back. The Cheyenne *were* on the warpath that fall and some of them, likely the band of Roman Nose, had tortured a young stockman to death and raped his wife and two little girls before killing them as well. So Colonel Chivington and the Third Colorado set out to pay the hostiles back, and at Sand Creek they shot the liver and lights out of the South Cheyenne camped yonder for the winter. There was nothing wrong with their intentions, and they killed as many Indians as they could in a proper military manner. Or leastways, they shot 'em up pretty good. Then they found out they'd attacked the wrong Indians. None of the Cheyenne camped along Sand Creek knew toad squat about the murders Chivington and the Third Colorado were sincerely out to avenge."

The reporter decided, "They should have been more careful, and what might all this stuff about the Colorado Militia have to do with more recent threats to blow things up around here?"

Longarm said, "Maybe nothing. Maybe somebody lick-ing wounds from the Lost Cause wants revenge, mayhaps for fun and profit. Professor MacLennon may be mad as a hatter or crazy like a fox, but he don't seem to be working alone. There's been rumors about a return of the notorious General Sibley. I find it more likely that some of those old boys who rode with him, and robbed every bank in Santa Fe whilst they was at it, might be plotting a return engagement. That might well explain two owlhoot riders, one of them called Reb, drifting in to Santa Fe spoiling for action, buying chaps for hard riding through chaparral and so on."

Lieutenant Lowell objected again. "A call for the South to rise again, at this late date? Let's be reasonable, Longarm. Nobody could possibly hope to put things back the way they were at this late date. The last Reconstruction ordinances have been set aside and most former rebels have settled down as law-abiding citizens these days."

Longarm smiled thinly and shot back, "Might you have any current address for them law-abiding citizens Frank and Jesse James? If you do, I'd sure like to serve a warrant on them for their own bank robberies since Appomattox. I never suggested any former Confederate field-grade officers might be backing the play of a disgruntled Confederate chemistry professor, Lieutenant. But ask yourself how many *thousand* irregulars rode with Sibley, and how close they came to *winning*. Then consider how old soldiers relive their victories and defeats, and ask yourself how many potential raiders you'd be talking about if even one in ten, or even a hundred, felt up to another try!"

"Try for what?" demanded a uniformed police captain. "We've been told this mad bomber from South Carolina has threatened to blow *people* up! What profit would there be in that to anyone with any sense of reason?"

Longarm answered simply, "I can't see none either. Yet somebody for some reason has to be backing the professor's play. He ain't all alone in a hill town, drooling over test tubes and writing threatening notes. Somebody's aiding and abetting him. Somebody capable of holding the whole town of Gilead hostage as they guard their chemistry teacher against the rest of us. No one man alone could come by the tons of potassium nitrate and barrels of glycerine it would take to booby-trap a town half the size of Gilead. So the professor has sold some others a bill of goods, or mayhaps they're using him, and his half-crazy skills, to further their own ends!"

"Which are?" asked Undersheriff Taylor thoughtfully.

To which Longarm could only reply, "I don't have the least notion. I reckon I'm just going to have to find out."

# Chapter 7

The coroner's verdict in the case of John Doe alias Samuel Adams was that the rascal had likely had it coming to him. So Longarm was free to go on about his business as long as he didn't make a habit of it around Santa Fe County.

Tess Bronson had allowed it might be best if she saw herself home after closing hours as usual so she could have a discreet supper waiting for Longarm when he arrived. That was what a spinster gal of good reputation called a supper on the sly—discreet.

So Lieutenant Lowell and another officer, a Captain Jolsen, were able to catch up with Longarm alone as he strode out across the plaza just as El Paseo was starting.

That was no place for three grown men to talk. So they moved over to a 'dobe arcade lit by hanging paper lanterns to make room for the local Mexicans out to get laid.

Lowell handed out one of those Havana claros he seemed so generous with, and the three of them lit up as half the single gals in Santa Fe strolled clockwise around the outside edges of the plaza while a whole lot of single and not-so-single men, Anglo as well as Mexican, got to moving counterclockwise against the current.

Captain Jolsen looked bemused, and asked if it was like that every evening in a greaser town.

Longarm got his cigar going and allowed, "Weather permitting. Some places the gals walk counterclockwise and the gents stroll the other way. It's the gals as set the local pattern."

Lieutenant Lowell said, "Captain Jolsen just rode in from Fort Union on advance recon. We were talking about what you'd said about those rebel raiders during the war. Didn't those Colorado Volunteers come through the Sangre de Cristos from Fort Union?"

Longarm nodded and said, "They had to. Started out from Camp Weld near Denver, marched down through Trinidad and over the Raton Pass along the eastern slopes of the Sangre De Cristos, and stayed at Fort Union long enough to rest a mite and pick up more rifle caps. As you both must know, you meet up with the east-west Santa Fe Trail a day's ride south of Fort Union, and follow her west a harder day's ride into Santa Fe through the southern Sangre de Cristos, unless you'd rather swing way wider through some mighty dusty arid range."

"What are those fool greasers up to?" asked the officer from other parts as a couple of *señoritas* passed them, giggling.

Lowell said, "Flirting. After one of them meets your eye and giggles more than once, you're allowed to look her up and down and smile back at her as if she's bare as a babe. If you show any interest any sooner, she'll take you for a jerk-off kid with no self-control, and we were talking about the route through the mountains from Fort Union."

The cavalry officer nodded and said, "We just rode over it. Where would you set an infernal machine to stop a column along that route, Deputy Long?"

Longarm had considered that, so he replied with no hesitation, "It won't work, Captain. They laid out the original Santa Fe Trail with easy travel for Conestoga freight wagons in mind. From the few times I've rid that route, knowing some of its history, I'd say Glorieta Pass was as tight a fit as you get along the main right-of-way. That supply column Chivington caught up with in Apache Canyon was trying to make a run around the Union forces blocking the easier path at Glorieta. If somebody else at this late date wanted to lead a column through the depths of Apache Pass, I reckon a few tons of high explosives buried in a canyon wall to either side could smart like hell. But the hills are too far back off the trail at Pigeon Ranch and Glorieta. You could bury your charge directly *under* the old wagon ruts, of course. But there's room for cavalry to advance in line-of-skirmish and you'd need swamping numbers, if not some field pieces, to hit 'em from either flank at Glorieta. Colonel Slough had more than a full regiment blocking Sibley's advance through Glorieta Pass, and it was still a hot contest. I can think of way better places to blow you gents up. I just can't see much *sense* in it. When were your troops fixing to leave for here, Captain? Or is that a military secret?"

The cavalry officer smiled at a lady with an organdy rose pinned to one hip and said, "It's neither secret nor definite. Like yourself, nobody at headquarters can decide which of several disgusting moves MacLennon might make makes any sense. That threat to roll a tank car filled with nitro-glycerine down the narrow-gauge into town is simply stupid. Need I count the ways a rolling tank car could be stopped on that long and gentle a grade, even drawn by a locomotive with some suicidal madman at the throttle?"

Longarm shook his head. "Not hardly. The railroad track crews all carry these simple gadgets to stop runaway rail cars. They call 'em derailers, because that's what they do when you set 'em on the track in front of a car you need to stop."

Lieutenant Lowell asked, "What if the whole thing is a

61

lunatic's raving rant and nobody is planning to do anything at all?"

Longarm said, "The professor ain't holding the whole town of Gilead in terror all by his fool self, and he wouldn't need to hold a town shipping potassium nitrate and glycerine in bulk in *any* state of mind if he didn't have something on *his* mind."

Captain Jolsen shrugged and said, "If worse comes to worst, I guess we'll just have to shell the place from a safe distance. Rough on the innocent bystanders, but to make an omelet you have to break a few eggs, right?"

Longarm snorted, "Well, sure you do, in an election year with the newspapers starting to print photographs with that new Ben Day process. If it wasn't for these other jaspers, who can't *all* be crazy, I'd suspect some sort of martyrdom by government gunfire was what he had in mind. For on the face of it, that's all a mad bomber can figure on, once he invites Presidents and Governors to come out and play!"

They agreed it was a poser, and parted friendly after Longarm said he had a prior supper engagement. As he was leaving the plaza, a really nice-looking Mex gal boldly called out, *"A 'onde va, vaquero?"*

It sure beat all how sharks smelled blood in the water and gals sensed a poor old boy's innocent intent. For he knew as surely as he knew the sun would rise again that had he had nobody in town to turn to, he'd be able to circle that infernal plaza all night in vain.

But Tess was waiting for him in her place by the river, with her hair let down and her kimono half open by the time they decided to skip dessert.

Later on, sharing a cheroot atop her rumpled bedding, Tess wanted to know why she couldn't ride over to Gilead with him in the morning, seeing she could likely get away with saying she was feeling too poorly to open the library.

He explained he meant to ride in the wee small hours

to begin with, and didn't see how she could pass for Mexican in the second. When she asked how long he meant to be there, he told her as truthfully that he had no idea.

He said, "I might be able to find out where Professor MacLennon is, if he ain't in that toolshed after all. If I can get him alone and get the drop on him, I could be back before this time tomorrow."

She asked, "What if he or his mysterious friends get the drop on *you,* Custis?"

He didn't answer. It was a foolish question and gals didn't like it when you laughed at them. So he just took a good drag on the cheroot and asked if she'd ever tried it with both her head and knees hanging off the far side of the bed.

Tess never had, or said she never had, and then they got a few short winks before the clocks tolled midnight and she served him ham and eggs with coffee and a blow job before she let him go.

He left a note with the night man at the sheriff's asking them to send his government saddle via his return ticket back to Denver, where it could wait for him in the baggage room and keep a few secrets.

Consuela was waiting out back of the *posada* with two scrub broncs, saddled Mexican with center-fire cinches and exposed cottonwood swells. Knowing he was reputed to ride a McClellan with a Winchester '74, and figuring he'd be working at close quarters in a tiny town, Longarm had elected to ride in packing no more than the six-gun you'd expect most hands to ride with and a derringer that was nobody's business but his own.

As they mounted up in the shadows of the stable, Consuela asked him who that *gringa rubia* who'd called on him earlier had been.

Longarm frowned down at her and truthfully replied, "I don't know any blonde Anglo gals in Santa Fe that well, *querida*. When did she come by and might she have offered you her name?"

The petite *mestiza* replied, "I was not the one she spoke with. Was Tio Paco she asked. He barely speaks English. When I saw her leaving I asked Tio Paco who she was. He told me she said she was looking for you, he thought. When he said you had moved out, she said that in that case she would ask at some of the other places in town. So tell me, did she ever find you?"

Longarm laughed and said, "If she had, I'd know who she was, right? I wasn't staying at another *posada* or any of those fancy hotels near the depot. That's likely why she never caught up with me."

"Do you not wish for to find out who she was before we ride out?" the curious Mex gal asked.

Longarm said, "If wishes were horses the beggars would ride, and you can only eat an apple one bite at a time. I can't hardly chase crazy chemists and mysterious blondes all at once, can I? They never sent me all this way after any blond gals. If she has anything important to say to me, it can likely wait until I get back to town. So why don't we ride and say no more about her for now?"

They did, and it took longer than expected. They were riding under a cloudless sunrise surrounded by dew-wet chaparral that smelled like a drugstore on a cool morning. With more of the same out ahead.

The Sierra Sangre de Cristo, or Sawteeth of the Blood of Christ, got its name from the way its jagged bloodred peaks loomed over the headwaters of the Rio Grande after high noon. With the sun behind the bald peaks instead of bouncing off them, the Sierra looked deep purple as they rode toward it at an angle. Consuela led the way to what he might have taken for a deer path veering off from Bishop's Road through the high chaparral. She said it was a goat path her own kind followed to Gilead. The high chaparral kept getting higher as they worked their way upslope. She explained how, even earlier than old Spanish times, some of her Indian ancestors had sheltered in those same bat caves during times of trouble.

The semi-literate Mexican gal who called a Confederate raider of her own childhood General Sí Sí had only vague family legends of times before the coming of the Santa Fe, or Holy Faith. But Longarm knew how the Na-déné, or so-called Apache-Navajo, bands drifting down from the far north must have terrorized the more advanced but less warlike Pueblo nations along the upper Rio Grande as they came out of nowhere, the way the Goths and Huns had come busting in on a dying Roman Empire a few years earlier. "Apache" simply meant "Enemy" in the Pima Pueblo dialect, while the so-called "Navajo" or farming Na-déné still called the extinct cliff dwellers they'd replaced the "Anasazi" or "Ancient Enemies." So it was easy to see how natives of these part might have kept handy hideouts in mind.

Consuela said Mexican guano diggers had sold out to Anglo miners and the bat-shit business had gotten much bigger. She said that once they had a modest mining camp going, it had followed as the night the day that Mexican farm and cattle folks had moved closer to a ready market for their produce. The notion of processing hides and tallow off surrounding ranchos had come with the railroad spur. Towns grew that way, out West or most anywhere that was handy for a town to sprout.

He didn't ask how come few Mexican New Mexicans marketed beef on the hoof to cattle buyers from back East. He already knew that you lost money on a market herd too small to pay the wages of your trail hands by the time they got it anywhere on the hoof to sell. One good trail hand could keep scores of half-wild longhorns moving more or less in the same direction. But he wanted at least a dollar a day to do so, driving them no more than fifteen miles a day if you didn't want them to lose weight along the way. So most smallholders, Mexican or Anglo, sold their cows closer to home for what they could get, and that made it profitable to run a modest tannery or rendering plant on out-of-the-way range near a railroad spur.

The trail Consuela had chosen suddenly opened upon a modest body of standing water too small to call a pond but too big to call a water hole. He figured the water was springing from under a big red boulder rising almost as high at the crack willows to either side. Consuela said it was a good place to enjoy a swim as well as a trail break, and seeing he hadn't had a chance to shower that morning, he thought it a grand notion as well.

But of course, once they got to splashing in the limpid springwater, Consuela wanted to try something she'd always wanted to do while swimming with a male partner, and though Longarm's spirit was as willing as most men's would have been splashing bare-ass with any gal built so fine, his flesh seemed a little weak where it really counted.

"What's the matter?" Consuela pouted, taking the matter limply in hand as she added, "Don't you like me anymore?"

Longarm kissed her, but murmured, "Hold the thought. One of them ponies just nickered."

Plastered wetly against him in the nude, the tawny little Mexican gal glanced over at their tethered ponies, placidly browsing the mesquite branches they were tied to, and added, "Is nothing wrong with *los caballos. Chinge me. Chinge me mucho!*"

He whispered, "Them ponies know one another well enough by now. So how come one of 'em just called a greeting?"

Self-consciously covering her bare breasts above the water, his bare swimming partner stared about, asking, "*A 'onde?* I see nobody. I hear nothing. Do you?"

Longarm eased over to the grassy bank to reach for his rolled-up gun rig as he quietly replied, "No. The son of a bitch seems to be out to sneak up on us!"

# Chapter 8

A million years went by as the sun rose higher and the skittering of lizards and such out on the chaparral made it unlikely anything bigger was moving enough to matter out yonder.

By this time Longarm and the girl had both dried naturally and put some clothes back on. Hunkered in the shade of a crack willow with Consuela, Longarm told her, "Stay put. Since the mountain won't come to Muhammad, we're just going to have to do this the spooky way!"

But as he crawled out through the chaparral like a sidewinder, it seemed whoever was out yonder felt even more spooked. Longarm circled to pick up nothing in the caliche or sunbaked crust between the roots of greasewood, sage, and such. The literal meaning of the Spanish word *chaparral* was scrub oak. In Old Spain it likely was. In the American Southwest you met up with about as much poison oak as scrub oak. So chaparral was more a stage of growth than a particular sticker-bush.

He found fresh horse apples on the goat path he and Consuela had ridden in along. Either one of their ponies or another pony entirely could have dropped them. The narrow churned-up strip of dust through the high chaparral didn't offer up particular hoofprints.

He rose to his feet for a better look about and, seeing nothing, muttered, "Up yours then," and headed back to rejoin Consuela. She asked if he'd seen anything, of course.

He said, "Nope. He must have heard that pony nicker too, and I do have a rep for being dangerous to sneak around. How do you like the same brave cuss who shot up my room at your *posada* yesterday?"

She said she didn't like it at all, and asked if he thought the jasper might be a friend of the one he'd shot it out with.

Longarm said, "It surely was no friend of *mine,* and they say the late Sam Adams had a pal he'd been drinking with in town before I showed up to upset him. We'd best be on our way, *querida.* How far might Gilead be now?"

She said they'd make it in less than two hours, and they did—a tad later than he'd planned, thanks to the delay by the pool. But it was still early morn, and nobody seemed to notice when the two of them rode in just behind a load of hay most likely bound for one of the livery stables in Gilead. They never asked the old Mexican driving the hay wain, and he never looked back.

When they got to a 'dobe half hidden from the road by a hedge of prickly pear, or tuna as *her* folks called it, Consuela led him around back, where they were greeted like long-lost kin by yapping yard dogs, clucking chickens, laughing kids, and a fat old *mestiza* who shyly said, *"Mi casa su casa, El Brazo Largo."*

Consuela introduced her as Tia Ynez. Ynez said her man was at work at the rendering plant. She had no idea whether he was rendering lard or glycerine at the moment. She said he had no choice in the matter, and advised them both to run like hell before those *tejanos* noticed them and put them to work.

Inside, having tortillas and beans with their coffee, Longarm and Consuela were filled in on recent disturbing events in Gilead.

The older *mestiza*, who'd been living there reasonably content, said the newcomers had simply arrived one morning about two weeks or so back. She couldn't say where they'd come from or how many there were because they shot people who asked such questions.

Longarm asked, "Are you sure of that, Tia Ynez? Can you say exactly who these Texans shot for certain?"

He wasn't too surprised when she made the sign of the cross and explained, "Is what I heard. The open mouth draws flies and the dead have so little for to say. Some say they are *tejanos*. They are neither of our own *raza* nor do they speak and act like most of the new Anglo railroad men and officials from the northeast. We have been told—we do not know anything for certain—their leader is a man of learning and that some of them rode with General Sí Sí that time they robbed all the banks in Santa Fe. They have spoken mostly to other Anglos in Gilead. You know how *tejanos* pretend the rest of us are not here. But everyone in Gilead is afraid of them. Very much afraid of them. It is said they have hidden bombs, big bombs, where only they and they alone may leave things as they are or blow them higher than the sky. Is better for to just do as they say and not argue with them, eh?"

She confirmed that for the most part the mad bomber and his followers had said to go on about business as usual. It seemed sort of spooky when you thought about a whole town getting up in the morning to spend the whole day scared shitless as everyone just went on as if nothing unusual might be going on. He muttered, "The crazy cuss is playing *dollhouse* with living souls! Let's have Mommy in the kitchen and Mimi upstairs making the beds, and if any of you dollies make me cross I might just bust your heads off!"

Tia Ynez signed and said, "They have told us you are most understanding, El Brazo Largo. But how are you to arrest them all without getting us all blown to bits?"

It was a good question. He knew better than to ask her where even one nitroglycerine charge might be planted. She'd said she and her fellow villagers didn't recall the gang infiltrating Gilead to begin with. They'd likely come in a few at a time aboard that narrow-gauge, or riding in in modest numbers, the way he and Consuela had just drifted in unobserved—he hoped.

He asked a lot more questions and got precious few answers as the morning wore on, with everything calm as a millpond and as tense as a cat outside a mouse hole.

Then the man of the house, Tio Carlos, came home for his noon dinner and siesta. Tio Carlos, like his wife, was past forty and running to lard. But he seemed a friendly cuss who wanted to help. The only problem was, he didn't seem to know shit.

He worked, he said, stripping fat from the insides of green hides in a shed between the slaughterhouse and his rendering plant. He had a hazy notion the wheelbarrows of trimmings he ran in to the cauldrons got to simmer down to liquid that more expert hands separated out, in some sort of fractional distillation, into different grades of candle tallow, castile soap base, frying grease, and sure enough, the sweet slippery baby oil called glycerine. Tio Carlos said that before the mysterious outsiders took over, the plant had shipped mostly candle dip and finished castile soap. The famous white soap of Castile was simple to make, although it required high-quality beef lard and the purest lye.

Longarm asked if they made their lye from sodium hydroxide or sodium nitrate.

Tio Carlos looked confused and asked what the difference was.

Longarm said, "I ain't certain. I ain't no chemist. I *think*

70

you make soap with hardware store lye, which is sodium hydroxide. But it does seem to me some of the elder folks back in the hills of West-by-God-Virginia used wood-ash lye, which was sodium potassium. Lord, I sure could use a chemist on our side right now. Have you ever seen them making soap lye out of sodium *nitrate* here in Gilead, *tio mio*?"

The Mexican shook his head and said, "Not where I work. I think I hear one of the *hombres* at the fertilzer plant saying something about this nitrate. You can make lye from this too?"

Longarm said, "Ain't certain. It's nitric *acid* I'm more worried about. As near as I can figure, if you stirred up an *alkaline* form of nitrate with glycerine, you'd wind up with a mess of *soft soap*. I don't know how you turn potassium nitrate into an acid or an alkali, and I don't reckon I ought to check a chemistry tome out of your Gilead Public Library if you have one. We were told the leader of this bunch, a Professor MacLennon, had been mixing chemicals out behind the *casa de gatas* run by a Madam Claudette. But he ain't there now. Can you suggest a better place to look for him, Tio Carlos?"

The local resident shook his head wistfully and said, "Madam Claudette does not entertain customers of *la raza*. So I had not even heard he was there. I have heard of this *bombadero loco*, of course. Everyone in Gilead walks in fear of his wrath. *Pero*, in God's truth, I have never laid eyes on him, or the General Sí Sí the others take orders from."

Longarm said, "Hold on. You don't mean Brigadier General Sibley at this late date, do you?"

Tio Carlos said, "I think that may be closer to his gringo name. As I said, I have yet to see him. They say he and the *bombadero loco* served together in that war about *los negros* a few years ago. They say that had they had some of his really big bombs with them that time they fought down in La Pasa Glorieta, they would have won. They say—"

Longarm cut him off with: "Never mind what they say." It was a waste of time to ask who "they" might be. Nobody ever seemed to know.

Fishing out his pocket watch, Longarm said, "It's going on quarter to two, Tio Carlos. How about showing me around over to your rendering plants whilst things ain't as busy over yonder."

The Mexican looked confused and replied, "Is siesta time."

Longarm nodded and insisted, "I just said that. Nobody will be there to ask you who I might be or why I seem so nosy. Hardly a soul ought to be on the street right now. I've often found *la siesta* a swell time to move across town on the sneak in broad daylight."

As they both rose, Tio Carlos laughed boyishly and allowed he'd heard El Brazo Largo seemed to become invisible from time to time.

So the two of them slipped out the back and followed a cinder path along the slope toward a not-too-distant and mighty high brick chimney. Glancing up at the red cliffs to the east, Longarm asked where the adits to the bat-shit mines were. The Mexican explained that while you couldn't see any from where they were at the moment, they were lined up under an overhanging cliff of red sandstone it was easy enough to make out. There were layers of shale, then a green cap of chaparral against the higher cliffs set back half a furlong from the closer rimrocks.

The burly Mexican led the way through a gap in a plank fence as he told Longarm it was a shortcut through a lumber yard. Longarm followed without argument to find himself, sure enough, threading his way behind Tio Carlos through house-sized stacks of milled lumber. They had barely made it to the far fence line when all hell busted loose behind them.

"Cover down!" snapped Longarm as he shoved the heavyset Mexican on around the corner of a lumber pile and followed, fast, then heard more gunplay.

"What is happening, El Brazo Largo?" asked Tio Carlos in a bewildered voice.

Longarm didn't sound much more certain when he replied, "Beats the shit out of me! Sounded like one pistol shot, two more from a bigger shotgun, and a fusillade of three or four more pistol shots!"

"Can you see who has been shooting at us?" the Mexican asked.

Longarm stared back the way they'd just come. There seemed to be a faint haze in the air well back. But that was all he could see from where they'd taken cover.

He confided, "I don't think anyone was shooting at us. I think we just heard a shoot-out on the far side of this lumber yard!"

Then a distant voice called out, "All clear. You can show yourself now, Longarm."

Longarm and Tio Carlos exchanged stricken glances. Longarm smiled thinly and murmured, "Not hardly. Recognize that voice, *tio mio*?"

The Mexican shook his head and murmured, "Is a gringo. That is all I can tell you about him."

The same voice called out, "We got him, Longarm. Stubby towheaded kid with a double ten-gauge Greener. I've never seen him before. Is he anybody you know?"

Longarm didn't answer.

The distant voice called out, "Oh, for Pete's sake, let's not play games with one another, Longarm! We knew you were coming long before you got here. We watched you ride in behind that hay wain with that Consuela Chavez, Tio Carlos's kinswoman from the city. We watched you go in and we watched you come out and it's a good thing for you we were watching, because this towheaded rascal with the Greener was about to clean your plow!"

Longarm put a finger to his lips and didn't answer.

The Texas accent in the distance had an edge to it now

as its owner called, "What are we trying to prove? We know where you and the greaser are, Longarm. This jasper following you with the ten-gauge was fixing to backshoot you when I shot him in the back instead. He got off both barrels on his way down, but I doubt he ever knew what hit him. It's usually a spine shot when their hats fly up like so."

Longarm didn't answer.

His unseen admirer called, "I answers to Jeff Moultry and I hail from Val Verde County, the Republic of Texas. I reckon you know who I'm riding with up this way. They say you're smart and it ain't no big secret. What say we all go over to the Apache Rest for some suds and a setdown in the shade now, hear?"

Longarm didn't answer. Tio Carlos whispered, "What are we going to do, El Brazo Largo? He knows where we are!"

Longarm muttered, "I noticed. In the meanwhile he can't gun us because he can't get at us, and sooner or later, that sun has to go back down, *tio mio*."

The older man laughed nervously and asked, "Are you serious? Is not yet three. Will not be dark for hours and we dare not move before then!"

"I just said that," Longarm growled, adding in a kindlier tone, "I'm open to suggestions, if you have anything better to suggest."

The Mexican didn't answer. Another voice called out from another direction, "You heard old Jeff, Longarm. He invited you polite to a set-down in the shade."

As they both turned to regard the surly-looking youth covering them with his Henry repeater from atop a lumber pile to their rear, the Mexican half sobbed, "*Madre de Dios!* They have circled us!"

To which Longarm could only reply as he put his own gun back in its holster, "They sure have. I wish people wouldn't do that, don't you, *tio mio*?"

# Chapter 9

The one they called Jeff had broken cover at the far side of the lumber yard with his own six-gun holstered. So Longarm stepped out in the open, and Tio Carlos gingerly followed, as that other one covered them from behind.

Longarm strode toward the mysterious Jeff Moultry, who got more lean and leathery as you neared him. He was dressed for riding, but fancier than Longarm, in black pants and a navy-blue shirt, with his black silk kerchief tied tight and worn like a necktie. His high-crowned Stetson Boss Model was mustard tan. His hatchet face was clean-shaven and suntanned enough to pass him as Comanche if he hadn't looked and talked so Texican.

As Longarm got within easy conversing distance, he told Moultry, "I thought somebody was shadowing us over from Santa Fe. You say he's a towhead?"

The tall Texican said, "See for yourself. He ain't one of our'n, and Old Sarge said not to let you come to no harm without he says so."

So Longarm joined Moultry at the corner of another lumber pile, and just on the far side sprawled a short pudgy hand, flat on his back with a dreamy smile on his face as he stared up at the sky. His hair was indeed almost

75

white. His hat lay yards away. His double-barreled Greener lay closer on the lumber yard's packed gravel. Longarm said, "Never seen him before. But yesterday morning I had to shoot another stranger who might have been a pal of his. He or somebody else with a shotgun shot the feathers out of my bed during *la siesta*. Fortunately, I was otherwise engaged."

Moultry quietly replied, "He was fixing to have another go at you just now. I reckon he thought he was the only one following you."

Longarm said, "I reckon so, and I'm much obliged. I . . . suppose you know that under ordinary conditions we'd have to report all this to the nearest coroner?"

Jeff Moultry nodded easily and said, "We aim to. Old Sarge likes to have as much law and order as the situation will allow. Let's go have that shady sit-down with some suds whilst my boys tidy up around here."

He started to lead the way. When both Longarm and Tio Carlos began to follow, the somewhat darker Texican told the Mexican, "You wasn't invited, greaser."

Longarm knew most Spanish-speaking gents would rather be called a motherfucker than dismissed as unimportant. So he quietly told Tio Carlos, in Spanish, how he wanted to handle things by himself.

Tio Carlos didn't argue. He just headed home, looking pissed.

Jeff Moultry led the way to the Apache Rest Saloon, a no-nonsense Anglo gin joint with no pretense at local color. Moultry led the way to a back room, and they sat on opposite sides of a card table whilst a nervous-looking barkeep with Irish features and brogue to match put a pitcher of suds and a fifth of bourbon between them, with extra glasses, before anybody had to tell him.

As Moultry poured, Longarm said, "I reckon you know why I tried to slip into town less dramatic. You must have more eyes on all the approaches than we figured."

Moultry shoved a schooner of lager and a tumbler of bourbon Longarm's way and laconically replied, "Field glasses, up on the rimrocks. Two hours on and one hour off. Day and night. Our observation post is connected by telegraph line to our command post below. Ain't no way a single schoolmarm on foot or a column of cavalry is going to sneak in on us across all that open range to the west."

Longarm sipped some bourbon and washed it down with suds before he reached for some smokes, murmuring, "I take it your leader, the Old Sarge, has spent time defending a naturally strong position before. What about the railroad line?"

Moultry said, "Old Sarge ain't our leader. He's our acting first sergeant. Weren't you never in any army at all?"

Longarm smiled thinly and replied, "I disremember which side I rode with during the war. It was long ago and I was young and foolish. But I did learn enough about soldiering to ask about that narrow-gauge line."

Jeff Moultry accepted the cheroot Longarm offered as he suggested, "Ask away. Then ask yourself how you'd sneak a railroad train, with or without troops on board, across wide-open range and maybe one or two little surprises planted under the right-of-way out yonder."

"With buried telegraph detonators," Longarm agreed, thumbnailing a match head to light them both.

He settled back and got his cheroot going before he sipped more suds and quietly said, "All right. You've convinced me you all have this one small corner of the universe by the balls. Would you care to tell me now just what the fuck is going on here in Gilead?"

Jeff Moultry said, "Ours not to reason why. Me and my West Texas boys just do as we're told."

"Which is?" Longarm insisted.

The tanned Texican looked a tad uncomfortable as he stubbornly replied, "Whatever Old Sarge tells us to do, of course. He runs things *tactical* around here. The colonel and the professor do all the *strategic* planning. Ain't you never heard of a chain of command?"

Longarm blew a thoughtful smoke ring, stared through it at the bottle of bourbon between them, and mused half to himself, "I have, and this one's pretty slick, if you're telling me true. Some former Confederate leaders have recruited the rest of you with promises of pie in the sky and a great day coming as long as you do exactly as you're told. Is that about it?"

Jeff Moultry looked away and growled, "Close enough. Thanks to the Damnyankees there's hardly any way for a poor honest rider to make his fortune off the land. But all a man needs to make a million is that first few thousand, and why should the nigger-loving Black Republican Damnyankees have all the money stored away where real men can't get *at* it?"

Longarm sipped more suds and muttered, "Aw, shit, I thought they'd sent me after a dangerous lunatic and you turn out to be holdup men! Who's this colonel selling you kids such sweet dreams? I know who the genius who came up with this pipe dream recruited as his chemistry teacher. So just betwixt you and me and your peerless leader, has he really got any bombs?"

Moultry confessed defensively, "The professor may be a little odd, but he knows his onions when it comes to stirring that bodacious nitroglycerine. Old Sarge says nitroglycerine is the stuff you make dynamite out of, only dynamite is weaker!"

Longarm grimaced and said, "Safer too. That's how come Mr. Al Nobel wound up so rich over to Sweden. Half a dozen chemists had blown themselves up with nitroglycerine before old Al learned to tame it by mixing it with clay and such so's it wouldn't slosh until you wanted it to go off. There must be plenty of clay in these hills.

78

The Pueblos still make clay pots in these parts and if you boys made *dynamite* bombs . . ."

"They ain't as awesome," the tanned Texican said. "Don't try to understand the method in the colonel's madness. He knows what he's doing. If he wanted anybody else to know, he'd *tell* 'em, wouldn't he?"

"Spoken like a true rider with the Light Brigade," Longarm said with a sigh, helping himself to more beer but easing off on the bourbon.

The door opened and another tanned rider under a high-crowned hat came in. He was older than anyone else there, and it showed in his iron-gray hair and snow-white mustache. The mousy little man in a snuff-brown suit he herded ahead of him was about forty, and seemed to be scared skinny about something.

Longarm wasn't surprised when Jeff Moultry said, "This here would be that lawman they told us to look out for, Sarge. I don't suppose the runner I sent for you explained how I had to gun that unfortunate following him and the greaser gal from the city?"

Old Sarge replied, "He did. You done right. Doc Townsend here has come to take your statement and issue a verdict of justifiable."

The mousy man, who turned out to be the town sawbones and deputy coroner for Gilead, didn't argue. He sat down, took out a standard form, and filled in the names without comment. Then he allowed everything seemed in order, and Old Sarge allowed him to leave.

Once the three of them were alone at the table, Old Sarge told Longarm, "We like to keep things lawful, out this way. Be sure you tell them that when you ride back to Santa Fe."

Longarm cautiously asked how soon he might look forward to that unexpected pleasure.

Old Sarge smiled expansively and said, "Soon as you've had your fill of sightseeing. They knew you'd be

79

coming. They told us to show you around. So finish your beer or bring it with you and let's get cracking."

As the three of them rose, with the liquor left on the table, the floor beneath them trembled and there came a thunderous rumble from, say, a mile away.

Old Sarge said, "Testing a new batch. We might as well start with that rendering plant you wanted to look over during this siesta time. Won't be no greasers working there at this hour."

As they were leaving, Jeff Moultry calmly told the older Texican, "He told that greaser Chavez to gather up all the women and children at his place and make a break for Santa Fe."

The Old Sarge shrugged and said, "It don't matter. They don't know anything as can hurt us."

As the three of them stepped out on the deserted main street, Jeff Moultry twitted, "Reckon you don't feel so smart about your Spanish now, eh?"

Longarm didn't answer. It would have been dumb to point out how Moultry had just warned him they both spoke some Spanish. A smarter cuss would have kept his mouth shut for now and told Old Sarge later.

As the three of them walked on toward that same brick chimney, Longarm idly asked if that mysterious colonel had a name, seeing they all knew who Professor Mac-Lennon was.

Old Sarge said, "When and if he wants you to know his name, you will hear his name. But not before. Suffice it for now that I rid with him as his first sergeant during the war and he knew his military onions better than some I could mention. We should have won, we would have won, had not some greener hands lost their nerve when that big bullet-proof Yankee major charged at 'em like a raving mad dog on horseback!"

"Then you were in the Battle of Glorieta Pass," Longarm decided.

To which Old Sarge grudgingly replied, "Not with the cowards who broke and *ran*! I was off to one flank on patrol when the shooting commenced. We naturally advanced on the sounds of the guns, but by the time we could get there, it was too late. A man can only do what he can do, and we didn't have enough ordnance *that* time."

They got to the rendering plant next to the tannery and, sure as shooting, they found nobody but a couple of watchmen lazing about. Or lazing about until Old Sarge waved them off and they lit out like spooked barnyard poultry.

As Longarm and the two Texicans strolled around inside amid smelly piles of beef scraps and ominously bubbling vats, Longarm asked how many pounds of suet you processed to get a gallon of glycerine.

The Old Sarge said "A lot, I reckon, but as you can plainly see, they run a heap of hide scrapings and beef trimmings through here. How many gallons of nitroglycerine do you need for a box of dynamite?"

Longarm grimaced and said, "Not many. I follow your drift. Professor MacLennon don't mix his nitroglycerine around here, I hope?"

Jeff Moultry volunteered, "Upslope in one of the mined-out caves. It's cool, underground, with nobody driving a wagon past to shake it. Once you blast the bat shit out of them old caves, there's more room than you can shake a stick at. Shitty bats have piled the dried guano ten or twelve feet thick in places, and every speck of that bat shit started out as *bugs*, caught by bats on the wing. Ain't it awesome to consider how many fucking bugs them bats must have et in all them thousands of years?"

Longarm shrugged and replied, "It ain't as if they had better things to do with their time on the wing. Where do you make the nitric acid out of bat shit?"

Old Sarge answered easily, "We don't. The professor

81

does. That is why the colonel puts up with some of his ranting and raving. Poor old cuss went mad over losing some gal after the South lost the war and all his sassy nigras ran away, see?"

Longarm didn't see. But he never told them Professor MacLennon's true love seemed to have things the other way around. Jeff Moultry had given away his knowledge of Spanish, or Border Mexican leastways. But sometimes a man who didn't have to sound as if he knew it all could find out a lot more by just keeping his mouth shut.

Longarm asked if they'd show him around that fertilizer processing plant. The Old Sarge said, "It's just on down the road a piece. You go on and poke through all that bat shit all you want. I can't abide the smell my ownself."

Jeff Moultry said, "Me neither. They serve a fair supper at the Apache Rest, unless you mean to spend the night at the Depot Hotel on the American plan, with grub throwed in."

"You mean I have the choice?" Longarm cautiously asked, watching for sneaky smiles as he persisted. "You don't care where I might or might not go from that fertilizer plant?"

Old Sarge said, "Come or go as you please, Longarm. We got no orders to stand in your way."

"What if I try to leave town?" Longarm asked with a frown.

Old Sarge said, "Whenever you like. You could ride back on that same pony, if the greasers have left any riding stock at the Chavez place. Otherwise, there's an afternoon freight coming in and heading back to Santa Fe as soon as it switches cars. We don't have a regular passenger line. But riding a boxcar for an hour or so never hurt a man with any sand in his craw."

Jeff Moultry volunteered, "If you decide to stay the night we'll doubtless see you around town this evening. Otherwise, if this is to be adios, then adios, old son."

And then they were walking away and Longarm was standing alone on the sunlit street feeling almost lonesome.

It had to be a trick. Not a thing he'd seen or been told in the town of Gilead made a lick of sense. But if this was a trick, what was the point of it and what in blue blazes was *going on* out this way?

# Chapter 10

Nobody Longarm talked to before or after the siesta ended that afternoon was able, or willing, to tell him. The notion he'd had in Santa Fe that the mad bomber and his gang were somehow holding a whole town hostage had to be amended, but not totally abandoned, as things seemed curiouser and curiouser the longer he was there.

Some folks didn't seem to want to talk to strangers in town at all. Others seemed polite, scared stiff, and unwilling or unable to tell him exactly what they were scared of.

The more he asked around, the less certain it became that they really knew. In that book about scaring folks by Mr. Machiavelli, Old Nick, as the author was known to his friends, had pointed out how most folks were more moved by fear than persuasion and how *not spelling out* just what you might do to them scared them worse than most threats you might come up with.

When asked directly, nobody said they were afraid to come and go as they pleased, although some recalled townsfolk who'd gone and never been heard from again.

Others, such as the railroad crews and riders off the surrounding produce farms and cattle spreads, seemed to move in and out of town as much as they needed to. Or as much as Old Sarge and his nameless colonel likely needed them to. A gang of undetermined numbers had to eat an undetermined amount of onions, ham, and eggs. It was easier to keep a whole town under an uncertain amount of control when nobody went hungry, thirsty, or unpaid. So Longarm began to see how this very laxity served to hold some folks tighter than armed guards might have.

As a soldier in his teens in a war long ago and far away, Longarm had seen who ran and who stayed put as the battle lines swept through a town. Unsupervised slaves, vagabonds, or poor whites with nothing to hold them within the sound of the guns lit out down the road while the going was good. Property owners tended to dig in and do what they could to defend their property. Local businessmen who depended on business as usual to make ends meet stayed open for business as long as the gunplay around them would let them. So it was way easier for somebody like Tio Carlos to abandon a shack and a low-paying job for the sake of his nerves. Folks in Gilead with a stake in the community seemed to be hanging on and hoping. The mysterious strangers had swept in overnight and might vanish overnight. In the meantime, they were riding in the driver's seat with a whip hand that sounded like distant thunder, but a fairly gentle hand on the reins, if one didn't mind an occasional suggestion and a tendency to eat, drink, and be merry without paying.

Both the tannery and rendering plant had been left to the original management, for the most part. From time to time the professor needed a whole lot of glycerine, and if he never seemed to pay for it, they were free to vend their other products to the outside world by narrow-gauge. When Longarm finally found a rendering gent who could offer a few figures, he discovered it was true you needed a whole lot of suet to extract a modest amount of sweet glycerine. But they were running a whole lot of suet through the plant, and nobody was stopping them from selling the rest. So who would want to abandon everything to wind up safe and poor in Santa Fe?

Merchants along the main street, not to mention the one bank in town, were still open for business because of the same simple logic. The gang had everyone spooked, and some saloon keepers and hash slingers outraged, but not to the point of either a mass stampede or a committed shoot-out. Aside from the tense atmosphere all the time, and those earthshaking rumbles now and again, business could be said to be booming just as much as those test explosions in the dinky town of Gilead!

Business would have been good in Gilead at that time of the year in any case. As most who made their daily bread off the land could tell new homesteaders, and often did, cattle and farming outfits inhaled and exhaled money in a different way than business outfits did. So the spring months, when cattlemen and farmers were spending money like it was going out of style, were the months you sold seed and supplies, trail provisions and such, and loaned out the most money for the same. The smallholders around Gilead weren't as boom-and-bust as bigger outfits such as the Jingle Bob and Maxwell Grant over on the Pecos. But they still needed seed, fertilizer, irrigation gear, and so on. So just then would have been a piss-poor time for a seed store or a fertilizer plant to drop everything and run. The one bank in town stayed open to extend modest loans against the fall payoff farmers and stockmen counted on. The uneasy banker Longarm talked to about that had decided a bank in the hand was worth two in the bush, and figured if those hard-eyed strangers in town meant to rob his bank, they'd have done so by now.

The same logic that kept most of the modest businesses in town open kept the two barbers, town sawbones cum deputy coroner, and of course Madam Claudette on call to serve the wage earners of Gilead.

Madam Claudette was a surprise to Longarm too. She was as blousy an old whore as he'd pictured, but more relaxed and easygoing about recent events in her toolshed than he'd been led to expect.

Entertaining him in her downstairs office when he politely declined a free roll in the feathers upstairs, the henna-rinsed and overweight old bawd poured Longarm Maryland rye when he allowed that was his pleasure, and handed him a heroic cigar to match her own before she leaned back against her rolltop desk with her robe hanging open to casually declare, "It's like I told them other lawmen, honey. I ain't got shit to hide. It's true Professor Norman MacLennon stayed here with us when he first come out here a month or so ago. It's true he was mixing some shit out back in the shed, and it's true I don't have the least notion why. I thought it was medicine. The poor cuss was a lunger as well as a sex-mad dope fiend. Lots of consumptives take more laudanum for the chest pains than they ought to, and whilst they can still breathe, the condition seems to make 'em horny as hell."

Longarm took a drag on the cigar she'd offered him. It wasn't easy to keep from retching. But he managed to sound comfortable as he said, "Some . . . friends of the professor have been wondering why he suddenly dropped everything and lit out for parts unknown. Could you pin me down some exact dates? Can you tell me when he got here and why he might have picked Gilead of all places, no offense?"

She absently scratched under a sweaty bare breast and replied, "None taken. I can't say exactly when he showed up on my doorstep—as a roomer, I mean. Some of my girls said he'd come by earlier as a customer with more passion than . . . equipment. You may find this hard to believe, but the life we lead gets tedious, with the New Mexico sunshine always much the same through the lace curtains and one damned cowboy or bat-shit miner after the other with the same requests. My girls like the cowboys better. Cowshit on one's boots is one hell of an improvement."

She could see Longarm was getting impatient. So she added, "Say he stayed with us about a month before that old army pal of his showed up."

"You mean the one they call the colonel?" Longarm asked.

Madam Claudette shrugged her massive shoulders and said, "Him too. Tall, lean, and mean-looking. Stayed outside like he was too good for us when he sent that one they call a sergeant in to fetch the poor sick bastard. They hired a private home on the south end of town, near the early bat-shit diggings. Caverns ahint the house cleaned out a long time ago, you understand. Every now and again they set off a charge under the mountain. Damned if I see why. Do you?"

Longarm shrugged and said, "The most common assumption is that the professor tests a batch of boom-juice down yonder from time to time."

"I wish he wouldn't." She sighed, explaining, "You get used to a little blasting deep in the bat-shit mines. They've been drilling in through the dried crud for years. But it only takes a little dynamite to shatter a day's mucking of bat shit. I've never wanted to go up yonder and look inside myself. But some of my girls have, as a lark, and they say it's the same color and about as hard as that paper machinery."

"You mean *papier-mâché,* ma'am?" he dryly asked.

She said, "That too. Only takes a little dynamite to bust loose a dozen tons. Lord knows what our Norman is out to blow up with those really thunderous bangs down the cliffs!"

Longarm truthfully told her he was still working on

that. Then he left to see if he could find out somewhere else in town.

They hadn't been able to tell him how you turned bat shit into nitric acid at the fertilizer plant. An Anglo straw boss of a mostly Mexican crew said the professor's mysterious pals were content to accept crude potassium nitrate or saltpeter leached from the raw guano in a tall wooden tank that reminded Longarm of the charcoal filter banks you ran rye whiskey through to clarify it. Although in this case the end result was a dry powder the color of dandruff instead of sweet-sipping Maryland rye. The straw boss, with about the same level of chemical know-how as the curious but semi-schooled Longarm, said he knew you could make gunpowder or nitric acid out of saltpeter. But he didn't know how, and wasn't sure he wanted to try. For so far, he had yet to see a fertilizer plant blow up.

Longarm had, but that had been ammonium nitrate, not potassium nitrate, so he felt no call to worry the cuss further. The straw boss told Longarm the one called Old Sarge had been buying all that Saltpeter with IOU's. When Longarm asked in whose name, he wasn't surprised to hear the Texas State Militia had been buying all sorts of stuff in Gilead on credit. All of the various state militias had of course been federalized as the jointly operated State and National Guard after the war, lest some future state government mobilize against the Union a second time. But if folks in Gilead were willing to extend credit to a nonexistent agency of a defeated rebel state, it was no skin off his own ass, and might save everyone a lot of bother.

Even as he came to this conclusion, Longarm had seen how the gentle reign of terror worked in Gilead. It was wrong, dead wrong, to buy on credit one didn't have. But then again, why challenge a man with a gun when he was smiling politely?

The narrow-gauge connections with the outside world

were simple but well thought out. The single line of tracks wound through the high chaparral from Santa Fe to the southwest to run along a more or less straight contour line a long city block or, say, six hundred feet downslope from the main street, with industrial plants, lumber yards, and such fronting on Main Street with their rail sidings to the railroad line. As he strode down to the dispatch shed and passenger-freight platform at the south end of the yards, Longarm saw a few boxcars and one ominous empty tank car parked on sidings to his right. But when he met the one grizzled dispatcher in the open door of his shed, Longarm learned the one and only daily train wouldn't get in for another couple of hours.

The uneasy-looking dispatcher allowed nobody had given him any orders one way or the other about the town's casual rail service. He said a Shay locomotive would steam in with, say, two boxcars and a caboose to unload any passengers, mail, and freight on yonder platform.

Then it would move on up the line, dropping off empties from the Santa Fe yards and picking up the filled cars waiting behind those bigger fertilizer and rendering plants, before it looped around on the far end of town to head back to the city. He said the lumber yard and the kerosene depot those distant cars were baking in the sun behind only needed a load of lumber or a tank car of kerosene now and again. He confirmed that as Longarm had suspected, that rusty black tank car stood empty at the moment. The dispatcher didn't know what they did up yonder at that kerosene depot most of the time. He said they were only open one day a week, selling lamp oil wholesale to stores along Main Street. The dispatcher thought the owners lived in Santa Fe and only rode out with a load of lamp oil now and again. He was certain the owners of the lumber yard spent most of their time on a country estate up the valley, far from the maddening crowd. Lots of bigwigs found the peace and quiet between Santa Fe and Taos to their liking because you could hardly get there from anywhere else. Anything or anybody serious from the outside world had to come in from the south: up the Rio Grande or over mountain passes to the southeast and southwest, with the passes between Gallup and Albuquerque, way downstream, even less convenient than the old Santa Fe Trail through the Sangre de Cristos.

Longarm idly wondered whose notion it had been to paint themselves into such a corner before they commenced to scare everyone else half to death. The more one heard about Professor Norman MacLennon, the more it seemed he needed his head examined. But why would even an old army comrade join him in a sort of blind alley with a whole bunch of boys out to do . . . something serious.

Even if they robbed one bank in a much bigger Santa Fe, with rail and telegraph connections General Sibley hadn't had to worry about, how were they supposed to get anywhere with their loot? Money in large amounts was heavy, and even if it hadn't been, what sense would there be in alerting the territorial and national governments that it might be a good notion to block the three main routes in or out of the Rio Grande headwaters?

He'd seen a single-strand telegraph line running alongside those narrow-gauge tracks, and the dispatcher had confirmed he was perforce in contact by railroad telegraph with the Santa Fe yards. Longarm hadn't seen any telegraph office along Main Street. But it was a tad early to wire his office in any case. Billy Vail could be such a pain about wasting the taxpayers' money, and if Longarm could get patched through to Western Union, it would cost him a nickel a word to say nothing all that much.

He'd passed the bitty hole-in-the-wall print shop twice before it occurred to him to peer in through the dusty glass. A paper sign said they were open and he saw movement in the back.

Better yet, another sign said they did job printing, and published something called the *Gilead Advertiser*. So it was likely what his pals at the *Rocky Mountain News* called a small-town boilerplate operation. It seemed surprising. But the mysterious colonel hadn't shut any other local businesses down, and next to a barbershop, there was no place in a small town better than the local newspaper to hear all the latest dirt.

# Chapter 11

Her name was Penelope Brite. She said her pals called her Penny. She stood tall for a woman, mostly on longer than usual legs, and her hair was the color of rusty bob-wire, including the traces of gray iron in places. He figured she was around forty-odd before she told him she was a widow running a boilerplate operation started by her late husband a few years back. The boyish figure under a denim work smock wasn't half bad, and aside from a determined chin, her well-preserved face was still girlish enough to make a man want to just drown himself in her big green eyes.

As they stood on either side of the counter running wall to wall between the front of her shop and the press room in back, Penny Brite confirmed she did indeed subscribe to a newspaper syndicate that sent her "Boilerplates" of *papier-mâché* she poured molten type-metal into for a made-up front and back page of national and international news. The syndicate set the type once, the regular way, and made the *papier-mâché* single-piece "Boilerplate" by pressing and ironing soggy wet paper over the set type. Pouring molten type-metal onto the two-page plate of *papier-mâché* didn't set it on fire because molten type-metal wasn't quite hot enough.

Penny Brite set the innards of her twelve-page paper, mostly offers to sell or buy, the old-fashioned way with a printer's stick. That was what she'd been doing in the back when he came in.

She seemed open and friendly, once he'd flashed his badge and identification, but as uneasy as everyone else in town about their recent arrivals.

She said, "I can't put my finger on it. Only one of them has ever spoken to me and they haven't threatened anyone in town directly. But you're so right about all of us running scared."

He asked about the one gang member who'd pestered her.

She said, "Pester might be too strong a word. It was that older one they call Old Sarge, a couple of days after we began to notice how many vaguely sinister strangers we had in Gilead of a sudden. I had naturally commented on so many apparent Texas cowboys this far from home during the spring roundup, and speculated as to who might ever pay some tabs they'd been running up."

She glanced past Longarm out the window at the empty street and continued. "Old Sarge was very polite. Almost courtly in that way some Southerners can put on when they have a mind to. He took his hat off as he looked around and allowed it worried him to think of a young widow woman all alone in here with nobody to protect her if some wild drunks commenced to shoot up the town. I asked him point-blank if he meant that as a threat, and he smiled in a fatherly way and asked why anyone would ever want to threaten such a pretty little thing. That was what he called me, a pretty little thing!"

Longarm smiled down at her and remarked, "You won't hear any argument from this child on that point, Miss Penny. But I follow your drift. The Mexicans call that sort of fighting the game of Tu Madre. Did I say anything about your mother? I have only the greatest respect for your mother. I would respect your father too, if anyone could name a father for such a fine *caballero*. The idea is to get the one you're bullying all steamed up whilst you just smile at him like the one in control. Over in New Orleans a spell back, I tangled with some Italian bullies who called themselves the Black Hand. They had everybody in the Latin Quarter scared and paying tribute. But if you tried to arrest a Black Hander, he'd just look innocent and ask the judge what he'd said or done wrong."

Penny Brite nodded soberly and said, "That's a very good description of the way this bunch has been acting. They don't have a particular title for themselves. Nobody knows exactly who their leader is or just how many of them there might be. The rest of us in Gilead just refer to them as *them*, and of course, one of them seems to be a crazy chemist who sets off nitroglycerine in caves from time to time. When you ask one of them what they mean to do with all that nitroglycerine, they say they can't rightly say. It's more frightening, in a way, than a direct threat to blow the bank vault down the street!"

Longarm nodded and said, "I suspect it's supposed to be. I spoke to your banker. They ain't even hit him for an unsecured loan, and he'd likely let the colonel *have* one, on the credit line of the dead and gone Texas State Militia. They've been playing Tu Madre with us all, inside and outside of Gilead."

She said, "I know. Albeit threatening to blow up Downtown Santa Fe with a giant bomb on wheels was hardly subtle. I suppose their leader, the mysterious colonel, would say he knew nothing about that if you tried to charge him with . . . what?"

Longarm said, "You suppose right, Miss Penny. The very purpose of all those threatening letters may be simply to establish their staff chemist as a hopeless maniac. To stick a legally sane leader with any hard time at all, we'd have to prove *he* meant it, and then we'd have to show he had a *motive* to mean it. Not even the mad bomber has made any demands for cash or kind. Telling the President you don't care for the way he's running things can be considered the private right, if not the duty, of any citizen. Telling the Governor of New Mexico Territory that you don't care for his biblical scholarship ain't, on the face of it, a felony."

She nodded and said, "I see what you mean. Writing anything to the late Robert E. Lee is not only silly but perfectly legal."

He cocked a brow to ask, "You know about all those loco letters the poor sick cuss has been mailing from here?"

She nodded and said, "The postmistress in the general store hasn't been opening his mail. The news service I subscribe to keeps me up to date on current events, and your mad bomber has been making the papers all across the country. Don't let this get out, but the news service always sends more details than we have space to run. So I've read the transcripts of the thirty or more mad letters he's sent so far."

"That's more than I have," Longarm marveled. "Might you have a private telegraph or one of them new Bell telephone lines, ma'am?"

She smiled and confessed, "Neither. Pop Wetzel, the railroad's dispatcher here in Gilead, patches me through to and from Western Union in Santa Fe when the line's not in use, which is most of the time. I have, let me think, thirty-two transcripts of letters sent out by poor Professor MacLennon, each and every one pathetic."

Longarm allowed he'd pay for her pile if she didn't aim to publish them line for line. He explained, "They only gave me transcripts of a few recent and more important-sounding threats. I've been trying to find some common thread to tie his delusions together."

She said she'd naturally typed carbons in triplicate, and moved gracefully from the counter to bend over and open a file drawer. She surely bent over swell.

Bringing a sheaf of onionskin paper back to the counter, Penny Brite said, "Maybe, on second thought, they get wilder as one reads on. The first letters he sent to people he seemed to like better. He allowed he'd gone out West to work on something bigger than he'd been up to as an explosives expert for the Confederacy. He said he was on to some discovery that would shake the world. And then he starts threatening to shake the world in less friendly letters to people he couldn't possibly have known back East."

Longarm rolled the sheaf up, and she handed him a rubber band from a counter drawer to keep it that way. He shoved the roll in a hip pocket as, off in the distance, a train whistle announced that afternoon run along the narrow-gauge.

The small-town newspaperwoman smiled wistfully and said, "I suppose you'll be reading those transcripts this evening in Santa Fe at some fine hotel?"

He said, "I ain't been staying at fine hotels in Santa Fe, ma'am. I ain't sure I'm ready to leave Gilead just yet. I ain't found out half of what I come to study on. But the trouble is, they know I'm in town and that can make studying them a bother. So I'm torn betwixt getting out whilst the getting is good, or finding someplace to lay low after that afternoon train leaves. If they failed to see me around town in the gloaming, they might think I'd given up and gone back to Santa Fe like all them other lawmen."

She nodded eagerly and confided, "We only have a few streetlamps along the main street out front, and my almanac promises the dark of the moon after sundown. But what if they have somebody watching the loading platform?"

He said, "If I don't seem to be around, once the train leaves, I could have boarded a boxcar, sneaky, up the line a ways. They're sure to scout around town for me in any case, at first. But as supper time gives way to sleepy time, they might let their guard down, and I can get around well enough by the dark of the moon. So I might hole up at the Chavez place. The strangers know nobody's supposed to be there right now because they were the ones who ran the family out of town."

She pointed out, "If they know the place is empty, they may have other uses for it. They seem to be headquartered in the Pedersen house at the south end of the mine works, and Fred Pedersen, one of the first settlers in Gilead, only moved away last winter."

Longarm smiled wistfully and decided, "You must creep about a lot by the dark of the moon, Miss Penny. But it don't look like rain, and I'll worry about where I might hide out after I lay some misdirections to make 'em think I'm gone. That's what this stage magician I used to know called getting folks to look the wrong way—misdirection."

She hesitated, then blurted out, "I work and live alone above this shop. My best friend in town, Sally Blair, moved into Santa Fe because that blasting down the way kept her awake."

"They've been blasting at night?" Longarm asked.

Penny Brite said, "No. But half expecting a sudden thump had poor Sally sleepless. My point is that you could . . . headquarter out of sight with me after that train left. I mean, I want to help in exchange for a newspaper scoop that could get me out of this one-horse town. I never offered to . . . you know, with anybody!"

He assured her he understood her good intentions, and while there was still time, headed back down to the railroad dispatch shed to sew some seeds of misdirection.

Longarm knew from his own legwork that one seldom

saw much with one's own eyes, and you often depended on what others told you *they* might have seen as you tried to put things together.

So he began by scouting up that dispatcher, busy talking to one of the brakemen from that train just up the line, and horned in to ask how much the fare to Santa Fe might be.

The dispatcher told the brakeman they were talking to the law. So the crew member snorted, "Leave your money in your jeans and just hop aboard afore we get to moving serious. Wouldn't pay the salary of a ticket puncher if we sold tickets for such a short run. We haul lots of freight and seldom more than two or three passengers at a time. So just stay out of our way aboard the train and we'll say no more about it, hear?"

Longarm pressed a cheroot on each of them, and ambled up the tracks toward the caboose in the middle distance for a ways. Then he stepped into some trackside ragweed as if to take a leak, and just kept going up the slope along the back side of a fence, until he'd casually crossed Main Street to approach Penny Brite's printing shop from the alley.

Hence later that evening, as the sun was painting the cliffs above bloodred, when Old Sarge asked Jeff Moultry, the younger rider reported with some confidence, "Must have gone back to Santa Fe, like they said."

Old Sarge pointed out, "They never said he'd gotten aboard that train. They said he'd been asking about the fare to Santa Fe."

Moultry insisted, "Now why would a man ask the fare to Santa Fe unless he intended to *go* to Santa Fe, Sarge? A couple of others I canvassed along the tracks saw Longarm headed along them toward the same damned train, and nobody's seen him anywheres around Gilead since the train left!"

Old Sarge said, "Look around town for him some more.

101

Try that Mex place again in case he's doubled back. We know they didn't leave him the pony and trail supplies he rid in with this morning. So he's going to get cold and hungry after dark."

Jeff Moultry grumbled, "So will we, sneaking around in the dark of the moon at this time of the year for a man having supper and a good night's sleep in Santa Fe!"

The older Texican grimaced and demanded, "If Longarm's having supper in Santa Fe, how come nobody saw him getting off the train in Santa Fe?"

Jeff Moultry looked confused, shrugged, and tried, "How in thunder should I know, Sarge? Nobody saw him get *on*. Maybe he got off just as sneaky. We were warned about that tall drink of water's sudden sneaky moves. The greasers say he can traipse around invisible, if he puts his mind to it."

Old Sarge insisted, "Nobody can be invisible. He can only stand in plain sight where assholes are too blind to look! So go out and *look* for him, you asshole!"

Jeff Moultry said, "I'll go. I'll look. But what if I just can't find him anywhere in Gilead, Sarge?"

The older rider patiently replied, "Then we'll know he's not in town, won't we? Get moving, soldier. You know this town better than any stranger to it. Put yourself in his boots and look for a place a stranger like you might grab a bite, a bed, or a piece of ass."

So Jeff Moultry went out on the streets of Gilead in the gathering dusk, along with some others, to scout all about for where a stranger in town might grab a bite, a bed, or a piece of ass.

They had no way of knowing that as they began their sweep, Longarm was biting into a steak smothered in onions by a hostess who was built even better in her housedress.

The other stuff, of course, could wait for later on that night.

# Chapter 12

It sure beat all how two strangers spending time alone together aboard a train, or hiding out after dark, could get to feeling as if they'd known one another longer. They'd agreed that out of sight was out of mind as things settled down for the night outside. So they talked considerably about the peculiar situation outside until they caught themselves talking in circles.

The only thing Longarm was sure of now was that the situation in Gilead looked tenser as one got away from it. The law in Santa Fe and the army further off at Fort Union had the citizens of Gilead living in mortal terror of a mad bomber. But closer in, Professor MacLennon seemed more a sick dope fiend under the wing of an old Confederate comrade. So, seeing that was all he was likely to know until he found out some more, Longarm changed the subject to the Widow Brite, her own pretty self. She wanted to know how come he was still single.

He told her truthfully enough, "I've been to too many lawmen's funerals to ask a lady to risk that much for the little I can provide, and if the pure truth be known, I ain't certain I'm ready to settle down just yet."

Pouring another coffee for him as she sat across the

table from him, she smiled knowingly and murmured, "Zim, zam, thank you, ma'am?"

He smiled sheepishly and replied, "Love 'em and leave 'em would be more my style, since you ask so direct. I *like* you ladies a heap, and parting can be such sweet sorrow when a man has a job as keeps him moving on like an old tumbleweed."

"You mean he has a good excuse," she chided. "I'm not saying that's right or wrong, Custis. A heart that's lived a bit can tell when it beats true or mayhaps just lonely, and there are advantages and disadvantages to happy-ever-after and we'll-meet-again. I've never told this to another living soul. Not a living *male* soul, at any rate. But a lot of us lonely widows have a sort of dirty little secret."

Longarm sipped some coffee, nodded, and said, "I suspect I've heard it. There's this young widow woman in Denver who's . . . poured more than one cup of coffee for me from time to time. She was sincerely upset when they lowered her rich mining man in the ground. She says from time to time she still misses him a heap. But there are other times she feels free to come or go to the opera or a dinner dance as she pleases, with no concerns as to who she might bump into or just when and where she might wake up in the morning."

Penny Brite stared off into space as she decided, "It's the *freedom* more than the desire to *do* anything in particular. The best marriage or most romantic love affair calls for give-and-take on both sides. A man or woman who's not willing to meet a lover halfway is . . . well, a lousy lover. But there are times, now and then, when you just don't *feel* like thinking about anybody but yourself!"

Longarm smiled knowingly and said, "I mind this old stockman I met up with a spell back. Lived alone in considerable luxury on a cattle spread big enough to call a state if it were back East. Said he'd been married thrice and lost count of the ladies he'd known less formal. Said he knew he could still have himself a pretty young gal to keep him fine company and bring him his pipe and slippers if he was ready to put up with all the chatter and think twice before he rode out to check his fence lines, shoot crows amongst the cottonwoods, or just coffee up with the boys at the crossroads store down the road a piece. He'd decided, seeing he had books he'd never read yet and knew how to cook for himself, he was likely better company for himself than any gal who'd have him."

The young widow laughed and asked, "What about his . . . natural needs?"

Longarm said, "I never asked. There's more than one way to skin that cat, but the Prophet Muhammad himself said it was best not to ask, since nine out of ten men acted silly from time to time and that tenth man was a liar."

Penny blushed a becoming shade and looked away. Longarm allowed it was about time he scouted down around that Pedersen place she'd said the strangers were using for their headquarters.

He eased out her back gate and started drifting in the dark. As many an infantry scout or Cheyenne horse thief could advise, standing tall and walking slow had dashing from cover to cover in a crouch beat by halves.

The human eye picks up rapid movement at the edge of vision in bad light, but tends to ignore upright blurs just standing there, or not moving enough to notice.

Also, there's a natural tendency to call out to another human from when it's not behaving in a menacing manner. But since Lord only knows what that flurry of motion at the shoulder level of a timber wolf might be, it might be best to shoot first and ask later.

So the tall deputy strolled slow and steady to a cross street, and drifted up it until he saw it led to a lantern-lit mine or cave adit he didn't want to pester.

He found a footpath along the base of the talus slope

or apron of fallen crud from the sandstone rimrocks above, and followed that at the same easy pace until the dimly lamplit windows of the Gothic Pedersen place loomed nearby. He drifted around behind, to find another somewhat wider path leading upslope toward yet another dimly lit opening in the red cliff. He was fixing to cross it and take cover behind the outhouse in the backyard when he heard a slight stirring nearby and froze beside a shoulder-height clump of prickly pear.

He heard the faint stirring again, along with the grating of steel-rimmed wheels on gravel, coming up from Main Street along that side of the Pedersen property.

An anxious voice across the way challenged, "Mississippi moonbeams, and who goes yonder?"

Another voice replied from lower down, "The Union cavalry at full charge, and what's the countersign, you asshole?"

The sentry posted cleverly near a backyard shithouse called back, "Moon over the Mississippi, the same as it's always been, and watch who you're calling an asshole, you asshole. What have you got there? More of that shit for the professor?"

The other man, pushing the handcart, snorted, "Why, no, I brought you some pickled pigs feet from the free-lunch counter at the Apache Rest. Of course it's the same shit, and I could use a hand getting it up the last yards of this fucking incline."

The sentry said, "My first general order is to walk this post in a military manner. Ain't nothing in my general orders about helping you with that dangerous shit. You just wheel it on up yonder your ownself and let me walk my post in a military manner, hear?"

The one pushing the load said, "Aw, come on, pard. This shit is really heavy, and they told you it ain't likely to blow up until after the professor fucks around with it."

There was a moment of dead silence. Then the sentry

decided, "Well, shit, if it blows up this close to the house and all that other nitro-whatever, we'll all go with it in any case. So let's get it on up yonder and safely underground for the professor to play with!"

As he heard the wheels grating on, Longarm took advantage of that to ease back the way he'd come. As he told Penny Brite once he got back to her printing shop, sneaking in the dark any closer to property guarded that tight was too big a boo.

When she sympathized with him for not being able to find out a whole lot, Longarm replied, removing his hat and rejoining her this time on a chesterfield sofa in her sitting room, "I found out more than they might have wanted me to. The professor does seem to be making nitroglycerine up behind the house in that abandoned bat cave. They do seem to be storing some of the end product in or under the house, and I wish I knew more about chemistry because they're supplying him with some secret ingredient I don't think we're supposed to know about."

She asked, "Didn't you say they were shaking down the rendering plant for glycerine and that fertilizer plant for saltpeter?"

He nodded and pointed out, "Openly. Not in secret, after dark. I just don't know what you need to turn potassium nitrate into nitric acid. I'm going to have to look that up. I remember reading *natural* nitric acid forms in the air to chew up statuary when lightning zaps through the natural air we breathe, which is more than half nitrogen gas. I read where some Dutch chemists have made a few drops of nitric acid by shooting electric arcs through bottles of compressed air. But it costs more to generate that much electricity than the end product is worth on the market."

She said, "Hold on. While you were out I went over some of those letters poor Professor MacLennon wrote, searching for that pattern you mentioned about his mysterious Jeremiah."

She rose gracefully to fetch the sheaf he'd left with her on the kitchen table as she called back, "I saw what you meant about his not-very-sensible references to all sorts of people and places named Jeremiah. But he's only done that in about a quarter of his crazy letters. Some of the other stuff he raves about reads even wilder!"

She sat down beside him again to shuffle through the transcripts as she said, "He did say something about nitrogen and electricity in more than one letter, now that you mention it. Isn't it sort of *dangerous* for us to go around breathing that explosive nitrogen gas all the time?"

Longarm replied in a surer tone, "Not hardly. I understand *that* part. Nitrogen ain't an explosive gas. Left to its druthers, it's what they call an *inert element*. It don't want to combine with other stuff to form other chemicals. Man and nature *can* combine nitrogen into nitrogen compounds, and most of them are explosive because the nitrogen wants to just let go of the stuff it's mixed with and go back to being just plain nitrogen, see?"

She didn't.

So he explained. "Chemical processes give off heat. Slow heat in the case of rusting, and sudden heat, a heap of sudden heat, when two or more chemicals rusted together kick loose from one another all at once. Common gunpowder is a blend of saltpeter or potassium nitrate, brimstone or sulfur, and willow charcoal. The nitrogen in that mix is ever ready to bust loose, and do you light a spark to start things off, it will. The nitrogen parts company with the potassium metal at white heat, which makes the brimstone burn like the very fires of Hell as it combines with the oxygen in the charcoal to go *gaboom*!"

She sniffed and replied, "If you say so. I only asked how we can *breathe* the stuff. I think this is the letter to another chemist back East in which Professor MacLennon brags about being on to a discovery to make his wartime efforts seem like child's play."

Longarm scanned the rambling note. He could see the professor had been drunk or full of opiates when he'd scrawled it, but this one was indeed more a brag than a threat. He was telling an associate at his college that he was working on a process out New Mexico way, while he recovered his health, that was going to make him rich beyond the dreams of young John D. Rockefeller of Ohio.

Longarm told the widow at his side, "John D. has made a name for himself peddling standardized lamp oil in considerable quantity. A man who could produce nitrates in bulk could write his own ticket."

She said, "Then that's what they're really working on in that mad scientist's secret laboratory, artificial nitrogen gas!"

He chuckled fondly and said, "There'd be more money in artificial nitrogen compounds, from fertilizers to explosives. I can see why the War Department is interested in this wild situation. But a scientist with a secret laboratory works better in a spooky novel than in real life. Neither Mr. Bell nor Mr. Edison are working in secret at the moment. They're having their new patent papers delivered to their laboratory's street address."

She pointed out, "Nobody's accused Alexander Graham Bell or Thomas Alva Edison of being mad scientists. Professor Norman MacLennon is as crazy as a loon! You can see how letters he posted right here in Gilead started out just a mite peculiar and then got crazier and crazier as time passed by."

"Time and consumption," Longarm soberly replied. He made a wry face and said, "Nobody wakes up one morning with the consumption. He was a young and healthy man during the war, and well enough to spark a right handsome lady of quality more recent. But he must have been denying a growing weakness that got worse and worse, until sometime last winter he had to face that he was really sick. So he headed west to the healing some find in the air out here, sipping more and more laudanum for the pain as he fought to find some way to make the money he needed without having to work at a regular job."

She said, "One of the first really bitter letters he wrote was to his doctor in Charleston, threatening to kill such a quack as soon as he felt a little stronger. Was the girl he'd been sparking a Miss Clovinia Cullpepper, Custis?"

Longarm nodded and said, "Yep. He wrote her a mighty cruel letter of renunciation."

She softly said, "I read it. He must have loved her very much."

Longarm started to tell her she was crazy. Then he nodded and said, "I reckon so. He sure made certain there was just no way the two of them were ever going to get back together. He must have wanted her to get over him sudden. But I ain't sure it worked. Like I said, she's a lady of quality."

Penny Brite said, "Well, *this* lady of quality has some galley to stick come morning, and it's way past her usual bedtime. Do you want us to go through the usual uncomfortable conventions, or would you like to bed down more comfortably . . . together?"

Longarm set the transcripts aside to take her in his arms as he gallantly replied, "Nobody but a total sissy would turn down an option so tempting, Miss Penny. But I hope you understand I only mean to be in town for as long as it takes to find out what in blue blazes might be going on around here!"

She demurely replied, "You'd spend the rest of the night on this chesterfield if I thought you meant to settle down in Gilead. I meant what I said about valuing my freedom after as happy a marriage as most. But as you and the Prophet Muhammad point out, people get silly when they spend *too* much time alone in bed!"

So he kissed her, and she kissed back in a manner to belie her claims of cool detachment. He picked her up to carry her into the bedroom. She was sobbing with desire as he lowered her to the bedcovers and began to unbutton her bodice.

She clutched at him wildly, husking, "Don't tease me this way, you brute! Show it hard and shove it to me without waiting to undress! We have all night to take these clothes off, once you make me come, and for God's sake do it *fast,* lest I come before you can get it *in!*"

# Chapter 13

She confessed she liked it even better with her duds off the next time he made her come. She mounted his naked body to gallop over the rainbow with him a third time, and then, of course, being a woman, she commenced to bawl like a babe lost in the woods.

Longarm didn't ask why as he got them both into a more comfortable position and lit a smoke for them to share. He'd slept with women on previous occasions. He just held her against his side and let her get it out as he did most of the smoking at first.

It worked. When she saw he wasn't going to ask, she wiped her eyes on an edge of the top sheet and said, "I'm sorry. I don't know what came over me just now, and whatever must you think of me?"

Longarm shrugged the bare shoulder under her rusty red hair and said soothingly, "That you're only human in spite of the grand way you screw, I reckon. I seldom sleep with men, so I just can't say how many of us men shed a few harmless tears at times such as these. I've noticed a lot of ladies do. I ain't sure whether it's a release of pent-up rage or confusion. None of us ever get exactly what we want because we all want the impossible. We all want a devoted lover willing to faithfully carry out our merest whim, forsaking all others and thinking only of us, and at the same time we want total freedom to use and abuse said love slave. Men dumb enough to ask at times like these are usually told they've used and abused a lady. I used to answer that I'd thought that was what they'd *wanted* me to do to them. But like I said, I don't ask no more. Ours not to reason why."

She suddenly laughed and reached for his limp virile member as she said, "You big oaf! You know very well it was my idea to seduce you just now."

"For which I shall be eternally grateful," Longarm gallantly replied as he placed the cheroot to her lips.

She took a drag, coughed, and asked, "Is there no end to the bad habits you're tempting me with? As a rule I don't smoke in bed."

Then she laughed wickedly and added, "As a rule I don't get laid so much either. I told you why. I'd be a liar if I said I hadn't been down the primrose path at all since my husband died, but only over in Santa Fe. There's no way a girl who wants to live alone in any town this size can invite a man to spend the night with her and feel sure he'll be leaving in the morning!"

As he took another drag on the cheroot, she stroked him fondly and explained, "Leaving sooner or later in the morning, I mean. You're going to want to hide out with me for at least a couple of days, right?"

He said, "I'm playing that by ear, with your permit. There's not much more I can hope to find out about a mad bomber and his mysterious associates up here above your printing shop. On the other hand, as soon as I show myself outside again, they'll know I'm still in town."

"What do you imagine they'll do about that?" she asked.

He said, "Can't say. I'll have to find out, unless I stay holed up until the afternoon train comes in and see if I can sneak aboard."

She began to stroke him hard as she purred, "That sounds safer, and I'm sure I can make you comfortable up here. Will you take me with you as far as Santa Fe, darling?"

She sensed the change in his breathing, and quickly added, "Only as far as Santa Fe. We settled that before we ever did this. But at the risk of offending your manhood, Custis, I've partly . . . teamed up with you like this to get shed of Gilead and all its memories of fair-to-middling sunny days and lonely nights under New Mexico's starry skies. Did you know a body could get nostalgic about drizzle?"

He laughed and said, "You don't need my help to hop a train for a short ride, Miss Penny. What's been holding you if you can't abide a fair-to-middling life in Gilead?"

She answered simply, "Traveling money and a lack of experience. I would need a new wardrobe and some time-biding money even if I had the credentials to ask for a job on a real newspaper in some big city such as Santa Fe or El Paso. But if I could put a real newspaper scoop on the nationwide wires, with the byline of my own paper's editor, I'm sure they'd give me a job, a real newspaper job, in the press room of a real newspaper!"

He allowed that sounded reasonable, and then, since she had him up to the occasion again, he snuffed out the smoke and rolled atop her to make her feel used and abused some more.

Before the night was over, Longarm was commencing to wonder who was using and abusing whom. But he forgave her when she served him ham and eggs in bed with plenty of genuine Arbuckle coffee to wake up on.

After a mighty friendly tub bath together, they got dressed so she could open for business downstairs. She pointed out—and he agreed—that a locksmith, sign painter, or printing shop shut on Saturday, when they did most of their business for other establishments along Main Street, might make those strangers curious.

But along about ten, having finished sticking and composing the last galley of her weekly paper, Penny allowed she might be able to pick up some news from the outside world from her pal the railroad dispatcher. So he put her printer's apron on over his shirt and jeans to mind the store while she was out. He doubted he'd be in any bind, unless some member of the quasi-military bunch came in to order some business cards. If one did, Longarm still had his gun on, under the apron.

None did. But in the short time Penny was out, he was able to swear the postman and two customers to secrecy and find out a little on his own about Gilead.

The postman said it had gotten its Old Testament name from some fancied resemblance to the Land of Gilead in the Good Book. Never having been there, the postman couldn't rightly say if Gilead, New Mexico Territory, bore any true resemblance to the real thing. But they said Governor Lew Wallace had traveled in the Holy Land, and the professor had told him he had things wrong about that in his popular book about Mr. Ben Hur.

Neither the postman nor the two businessmen leaving print orders for Penny Brite had heard for *certain* of any infernal devices planted in or about Gilead. Members of the professor's whatever had only *hinted* there might be, the way those Black Handers in New Orleans had only hinted a market stall might catch fire or tip over some night if the owner didn't think he needed their "protection." But nobody in Gilead had been shaken down for cash. So far. Some of the tabs the bunch had run up for food, fun, and industrial chemicals were making townsfolk mighty thoughtful, but not ready to take anyone with so many friends to court just yet.

Penny came back, bursting with news from the railroad telegraph out of Santa Fe. They listened in on Western Union over in the telegraph shack in the Santa Fe yards when railroad dispatching was slow.

She said, "Professor MacLennon sent an open challenge to the U.S. Cav at Fort Union. He must have posted it just before you arrived. He says he's been expecting them and preparing a hot reception for what he only starts to describe as Damnyankee Niggerlovers. I wasn't able to get Pop to tell me the exact words. But I asked and, sure enough, the mad bomber *does* rave some more about that mysterious Jeremiah in his latest missive. Let's close for *la siesta* and go back upstairs."

He said, "I was about to suggest that. But what did he say about old Jeremiah this time?"

Turning the sign in her window glass and locking the front door, she said, "Nothing sensible. Pop says there's no Jeremiah Pass over the Sangre de Cristos, and he would know, having driven a freight wagon on the old Santa Fe Trail before they laid those rails along it."

As he followed her upstairs, she continued. "The threatening letter said they'd find he was right whether they moved west through Apache, Glorieta, or Jeremiah Passes. Pop says he never heard of a Jeremiah Pass down that way."

Longarm said, "By Jimmies, I'd clean forgot the Atchison, Topeka, and the Santa Fe! Them new tracks *do* run through the Sangre de Cristos, I just rode along 'em on the train the other day! I must have rid through that old battlefield and never *thought* about Glorieta Pass and such! They have a big park blanketing the site of the Battle of Long Island these days, and some say you can drive through the old battlefield at Shiloh and see nothing but fruit trees now. I ought to be whipped with snakes, but all this time I've been picturing empty mountain passes. But I just now remembered stopping for engine water at a stop called *Glorieta*! That's likely close to where they had the battle when the world was younger and not so cluttered!"

He moved to an upstairs front window to stare out at

the view to the west. It wasn't far different from the view from an upstairs window of another independent widow woman on Denver's Capitol Hill. The high sun was painting the more distant Sierra Nacimentos, or main ridge of the Continental Divide, a soft hazy lavender. Like the nearby Sangre de Cristos, the Nacimentos ran more or less north and south as offshoots of the complex called the Rocky Mountains. The high red Sangre de Cristos were a sort of bodacious southern extension of the hogback "Redrocks" between Denver and the higher Rockies to the west. The jumble of upthrust granite and sedimentary rock got lower, wider, and more complicated running south, with the jaggedy Sierra Sangre de Cristos spread out from the main ranges like a big stone splinter, still attached at the high north end, to form a big blind alley to the north.

Turning to Penny Brite with a puzzled smile, Longarm said, "He *must* be mad and I sure feel dumb, picturing all them soldiers blue riding around the mountains on horseback when they can simply ride the train!"

"All the way from Fort Union?" she asked uncertainly.

Longarm thought and said, "Not all the way. One hard day's ride down the far side of the Sangre de Cristos to that railroad stop at Las Vegas, where the AT&SF crossed soggy bottomlands. Las Vegas means The Meadowlands in Spanish. Once they get there, they can load their mounts, their field pieces, and such aboard boxcars and ride through that old battlefield at Glorieta Pass in . . . Hold on! That don't look so good!"

She asked what he was worried about.

He said, "Glorieta Pass. I dismissed the notion of an ambush there by less than a division because the pass is so wide you hardly know you're going through the southern foothills of the Sangre de Cristos. But an infernal device placed under a *railroad track,* anywheres betwixt Las Vegas and Santa Fe, would be another matter entire!"

She proved she had the makings of a big-city reporting

gal by asking why they'd want to warn the army those mountain passes were dangerous. She said, "The others have to know he's been sending those threatening letters. They've been making it to the news wires!"

Longarm nodded and said, "The others I've spoken to sound more levelheaded too. It might be meant to discourage the troops from hopping the AT&SF through the mountains. Take 'em another full day in the saddle if they rode, deployed in a safer line of skirmish. But then what? Sooner or later they'd still get here, mad as hornets about the professor's dare, with enough artillery and manpower to seal off the whole upper valley and bottle the whole bunch up!"

She asked, "Would you be terribly upset if I just gave you a blow job and went to get my pony whilst the streets are deserted?"

He said he could survive without an orgasm for a spell, and asked where she meant to ride her pony.

She said, "Into Santa Fe. You're welcome to ride with me. I wish you would. There's nothing either of us can do here in Gilead but *wait*. The action will be riding into Santa Fe from the southeast!"

"If there's going to be any action," Longarm pointed out with a dubious smile. "Any troop commander worth his salt can see just as I can that MacLennon and his pals *want* the troops from Fort Union to head this way. If we can see how easy it would be to plant a nitroglycerine bomb under the tracks, those army men ought to see it too. So like us, they're going to puzzle some before they make their next move."

She insisted, "Whatever their next move may be, they'll move up through Santa Fe before they get here, and I want to put what I have on the wire with my byline!"

Longarm didn't argue, seeing she was so bound and determined. He kissed her adios in a brotherly way after declining her second invitation to ride in with her.

After she left, he went through her reference books downstairs in search of any town in New Mexico Territory called Jeremiah. He didn't find any. He hadn't expected to. Penny Brite didn't have any books on mental problems. She likely didn't hold with Darwin on evolution or Gladstone on freeing Ireland and reforming whores either.

He didn't open for business as *la siesta* ended. He'd long since regretted not riding into Santa Fe with a gal who'd offered to blow him, for he sensed she'd been right and he was just chasing his own tail here in Gilead, waiting for something new to take place.

So when the narrow-gauge Shay pulled in that afternoon, Longarm took a deep breath, straightened his hat, adjusted his six-gun, and headed on down to the tracks.

Nobody seemed to notice. As he strode down the slope, a brass band had just finished playing "Dixie" on the loading platform. Longarm was sure their nice gesture hadn't been meant for him.

He knew that was true as he drifted through the gathering crowd to see Jeff Moultry and some others now in Confederate gray loading a honey-blonde and her traveling bags into a nearby coach and four.

It was Clovinia Cullpepper. He'd been afraid it might be the gal who'd come calling at his *posada* in Santa Fe.

Worse yet, as Longarm slowly crawfished back through the crowd, she spotted him and called out, "Deputy Long! I was looking all over Santa Fe for you. So when they told me you were here, I knew it was safe to come all the way."

Longarm could only stand there like a big-ass bird as the innocent little thing trilled on. "These old war comrades of Norman have come to carry me to him. Why don't you come along? Won't you come along?"

Longarm didn't answer. Longarm didn't have to answer as Jeff Moultry politely but firmly called out, "You heard the lady, friend. Why don't you just come over here and join us in this carriage, like the lady invited you to!"

120

# Chapter 14

Longarm got in beside Clovinia Cullpepper, facing forward. Jeff Moultry got in to ride backward, facing them. The eight men with him mounted up to follow on horseback. The entire impressive honor guard was in Confederate dress gray, or as close as most irregulars had ever gotten to it in wartime. Jeff Moultry wore gold corporal's stripes on his gray sleeves, and the pants he'd donned for the occasion were at least a charcoal gray. His Texican Stetson was the same mustard tan as ever.

The brass band, recruited from the Gilead Fire Volunteers, was in Union blue as they sent the carriage on its way with another chorus of "Dixie." Longarm doubted they had the sheet music. But everybody knew how "Dixie" went, and so only the tuba flatted out near the end.

Longarm knew where they had to be headed. But Clovinia didn't, so she asked. Jeff Moultry politely replied, "GHQ in a commandeered mansion, Miss Clo. The colonel is out of town inspecting the enemy approaches at the moment, and I fear your Professor MacLennon is . . . ah, indisposed at the moment. The news of your pending arrival seems to have . . . overexcited him."

Longarm said just as politely, "He means your Norman celebrated ahead of time with that medicine he takes a lot, Miss Clo."

Then he asked the "corporal" if his colonel might be down around Jeremiah Pass at the moment.

Moultry looked sincerely confused, and asked, "Is that supposed to be funny? Never heard of no Jeremiah Pass in these hills. Ain't Jeremiah a name from the Good Book? Wasn't it Jeremiah fit the Battle of Jericho?"

Longarm said, "That was Joshua. Jeremiah was a prophet and a real fuss, now that some of it comes back to me. Don't read the Good Book regular. But in my day in West-by-God-Virginia, they sure pounded a heap of it into us at Sunday school."

Clo blinked and said, "Oh, I remember the Prophet Jeremiah now! He was the one who raved and ranted at the Children of Israel because he couldn't get them to change their ways, right?"

Longarm nodded soberly and said, "That's how come they call a long nagging political speech a jeremiad to this day."

She asked, "Might not that mean that my Norman's harping on the name of Jeremiah means he's unconsciously demanding we all change our ways?"

Jeff Moultry asked what she meant about the professor harping on the Prophet Jeremiah. Before she could say too much, Longarm casually explained, "He's slipped up a few times and called somebody Jeremiah instead of what he meant to call them, most likely. You know how old Norm gets when he's . . . excited."

Moultry dropped it as they pulled into the drive of the Pedersen place. By daylight Longarm saw the Gothic pile was painted park-bench green with salmon trim, as if to make it stand out against the red sandstone cliffs behind it. This late in the afternoon the Sangre de Cristos were living up to their name as to both color and sticky temperature. Jeff Moultry promised it would be cooler inside. As Longarm helped Clo down from the carriage, Old Sarge came out on the veranda in his own version of Confederate dress gray, complete with gold cavalry stripes down the dark gray pants. Longarm figured they had started out as Mexican Lancer pants. Lots of old Texican families had such souvenirs in the attic. The cavalry saber Old Sarge had on was real Confederate issue, though. He'd either picked it up in a San Antonio hockshop or kept it from his days at Glorieta.

Sweeping off the real Confederate cavalry hat he'd rummaged somewhere, Old Sarge exclaimed, "The professor failed to do you justice, ma'am. He only told us you were the fairest belle in the Carolinas. We have your suite prepared up under the mansard where there's a cross breeze, and the boys will carry your stuff on up, so if you'd care to follow, we'll do out best to make you comfortable after your long and weary trip!"

As Longarm tagged along, Clo said, "I only came down from Denver. I've been staying there with this sweet old couple Custis here left me with. I came down to show him another letter from Norman, forwarded to me from home. How did you gentlemen know I was coming here to Gilead? In his last letter Norman warned me not to."

On the stairs, Old Sarge conceded, "The professor gets to writing all sorts of things late at night when he's . . . weary-headed, Miss Clo. But of course he was delighted to hear you were in Santa Fe looking for him."

Clo started to say she'd actually been looking for someone else, but desisted after Longarm pinched her elbow hard. That was an edge a man had when he was helping a lady up a flight of stairs.

The long-gone Pedersens had surely sold enough bat shit to build a mess of stairs. But at last Old Sarge led them into a corner room with two oval windows set at right angles in its inward-slanting walls, papered with purple pansies on a tangerine background, and furnished grandly in mock Louis XVI style, with the gilt four-poster scandalous even for a New Orleans parlor house.

Old Sarge made a sweeping gesture with his doffed hat and told her to make herself at home. He added that the *chicas* were filling a tub bath for her next door, and motioned Longarm to follow as he turned to bow his courtly self out.

But Clo said, "I want Deputy Long to stay a few minutes. I've come so far and we've so much to talk about."

Old Sarge said, "Your wish is our command, ma'am, compliments of the colonel. But we're still fixing to serve supper downstairs just after sundown, and we hope to have your betrothed in shape to greet you properly by then."

He bowed himself out. As soon as they were alone, she asked Longarm if they might mean her Norman was drunk.

Longarm said, "No might about it, Miss Clo, albeit to be fair, they say the opium in them laudanum spirits can confound the mind worse than the alcohol. I sure wish you'd stayed in Denver, ma'am. But you said you had something new to tell me?"

She said, "Yes. In his last letter Norman tells me he means to go live in Constantinople where the Turks know how a natural man with a . . . never mind, should live. That's just him being silly again. But he did confide the Grand Turk would surely reward him beyond the dream of Ali Baba for the secret of making nitric acid out of pure air. He said you use nitric acid to make all sorts of explosives, medicines, and dyes, but the methods everyone has always had to use are dreadfully expensive."

Longarm said, "So I hear tell. Turning the nitrogen in the air all around to nitric acid would surely rate a handsome reward from the Grand Turk, the Czar of All the

124

Russians, or for that matter, Queen Victoria. Al Nobel wound up rich as anything just for inventing a way to handle one nitric acid compound without getting killed. I sure wish I had a basic chemistry book right now."

She leaned closer to confide, "You will have, as soon as they bring my bags up. That dear old fuss Marshal Vail had that nice boy Henry buy me a schoolbook on basic chemistry. Wasn't that thoughtful of them?"

Longarm laughed incredulously and declared, "I can see what my boss was fussing about. I should have brung one along. But how was I to know your intended thought he was on to a whole new way of making nitric acid to make nitroglycerine?"

A few minutes later some servants carried Clo's two bags in and scurried off, not being members of the inner circle and feeling spooked by anyone fixing to have supper with the same.

So a few minutes after that, when a cuss wearing dress gray and a Colt Lightning came to tell Longarm his own quarters were ready if he knew what was good for him, Longarm had the cloth-bound schoolbook tucked in his belt under his shirt and went along quietly, after telling Clo he hoped to see her at supper. It wasn't clear whether they were prisoners or not. The game of Tu Madre was designed to keep one guessing.

Once he was alone behind closed doors with that schoolbook, it only took a few minutes to wonder whether the professor was confused about making oil of vitriol or *sulfuric* acid from thin air.

Thin air, water, and fuming brimstone or high sulfur coal, that is. There was a simple diagram in the book showing how commercial amounts of $H_2SO_4$ or sulfuric acid could be made in a long inclined tunnel with a lead sheet or glazed tile lining. Sulfuric acid formed naturally and played hob with the stonework of big coal-burning cities like London when the sulfur fumes given off by burning too much coal mixed with the water and oxygen in the air. So if you filled your sloping tunnel with sulfur smoke or, in a pinch, soft coal smoke, then shot some hot steam up it, the acid condensed on the lining to trickle down where it could be funneled into a container.

Once you had enough oil of vitriol, it was simple to get $HNO_3$ or nitric acid to make explosives and other good things out of.

You trickled your sulfuric acid through saltpeter or any nitrate salt with metallic mollyboogers in it through a filter of platinum mesh. The only part that was expensive was that special platinum filter they made for chemistry labs, and you could use it over and over because it was called a catalyst and only greased the skids for the boogers without getting used up.

It seemed tedious, but if you had the patience and the time, the book explained how the boogers of sulfur liked the boogers of potassium better and eloped from the wet mix to form solid potassium sulfide.

This left the nitrogen boogers nowhere to go but into the acid mix of hydrogen and oxygen boogers. So that was what it did, and you wound up with $HNO_3$ or nitric acid. Not directly from thin air, as the professor bragged, but he had a Jeremiah Pass through the Sangre de Cristos, so what the hell.

It seemed complicated and time-consuming for the end results, but they'd been calling MacLennon a mad bomber. His mysterious pals might or might not know you could turn downright dangerous nitroglycerine to safer dynamite just by mixing it with fuller's earth or most any other inert shit, including shit, to keep it from sloshing as you moved it about. It was sloshing nitroglycerine that set it off. Handling the stuff in liquid form was more dangerous than juggling busted glass. You only cut your hand to the bone messing round with busted glass.

One of the scared-looking servants that they'd dragooned, this one a Mexican kid, came to tell Longarm supper was about to be served. So Longarm followed, hat in hand and gun on hip, because a man just never knew when he might want to make a break for it. He hid the book under the mattress of the more modest bedstead in his room.

Down in the main dining room, Longarm found Clovinia Cullpepper already at the table, with Jeff Moultry seated to one side and Old Sarge across from her. There was an empty space at the head of the table as well as next to Clo. Longarm modestly took that one. He felt sure the place of honor was reserved for the colonel or the professor. Three lesser lights occupied the other places at the table. It was set with that odd mixture of crude and fancy ware you noticed in outlaw camps and guerrilla garrisons. Riders who neither paid for anything nor took anything with them didn't worry about matching silver services or napery. Another proddy servant had poured red wine in a mixed set of glasses at each setting. Longarm had eaten in enough fancy homes to know you didn't serve the main course until the host or guest of honor had been seated.

Clo leaned closer to murmur, "Custis, they seem to think I'm here to . . . marry Norman!"

He dryly asked, "Ain't you? I asked you to stay in Denver and wait till I found out what was going on. Don't you like old Norm no more?"

She confided, "I don't know. I guess so. I mean, we were engaged and all. But he's been acting so odd and these men . . . have on Confederate uniforms and talk so mysterious!"

Old Sarge, across the way, calmly said, "There's no mystery, Miss Clo. Colonel's orders. He feels that since the professor is so fond of you and you seem so interested in him, the colonel would feel more comfortable if the two of you were married up. So we've sent for the justice of the peace, and your groom-to-be should be down from his quarters any minute now."

Longarm had no safe way to tell the bewildered gal a wife wasn't allowed to testify against her husband, according to the mythology of the owlhoot trail. Telling her this would have only upset her, and in point of fact it wasn't true.

The letter of the law read that a wife could not be *compelled* to testify against her husband against her will. If she *wanted* to tell the judge and jury the crazy bastard was mixing nitroglycerine out back, she'd have every right to.

Marriages entered into under duress didn't count either. So when Old Sarge suggested they'd be honored to have a Black Republican lawman as a witness, Longarm simply replied he'd be proud to sign anything but an IOU for them. He could tell Old Sarge thought he was afraid of him. Old Sarge, like a lot of natural bullies, was inclined to put too much stock in his posturing.

There was a stir at the far end of the room, and two more whatevers in dress gray came in with a cadaverous figure in a loose black suit held up between them. You could see the poor cuss had been nice-looking in his day. But now his sunken face was ashen where it wasn't an unhealthy shade of puce, and his lank dark hair was starting to go gray.

At Longarm's side, Clo gasped, "Norman, dear heart, what have you done to yourself?"

Professor Norman MacLennon stared owlishly their way and croaked like a singing frog, "Well, I fucked her laying and I fucked her lying, and if she'd have had wings I'd have fucked her flying. But what the fuck are *you* doing here, Miss Clo? Didn't you get my last letter?"

The abashed honey-blonde covered her red face with a napkin.

Old Sarge said, "She's come to marry up with you, Professor. Won't that be nice?"

The consumptive drunk stared thunderstruck and wailed, "I can't get married. Not to Miss Clo. Not to nobody. I got a dreadful cough that's catching, and it burns like fire when I pee. Let me go back upstairs, boys, I'm starting to feel poorly!"

Old Sarge took off the velvet glove and said, "Sit him down in his chair. I'm hungry, and as soon as they get here with that JP, we'll marry them up and have our damn supper!"

The men holding the professor shoved him roughly down in his place of honor as Clo wailed, "Don't maul him like that! Can't you see he's been ill?"

Professor MacLennon snatched up his wine, swallowed it at a gulp, and gasped, "You don't know the half of it, my darling Miss Clovinia. Yeah, though I walk through the shadow of the valley of evil, I find it scary as hell and nothing I can do about it makes it any better!"

Old Sarge said soothingly, "Take it easy, Professor. We'll have you fixed up with your true love in your bridal suite in no time!"

# Chapter 15

Some others in dress gray showed up with a justice of the peace from Gilead a few minutes later. The JP looked as uneasy as the servants, but seemed no more anxious than they to dispute the authority of Old Sarge.

The informally appointed first sergeant of what Longarm estimated to be about a platoon of, say, thirty rose from the table to propose they hold the ceremony in the parlor across the central hall. So there was considerable confusion getting everyone into the other room, and the professor seemed to have passed out along the way.

Longarm found himself alone on a window seat with the bewildered blonde, the both of them ignored for the moment as the others tried to bring the professor around so he could marry Clo.

She whispered, "I can't marry Norman in his present condition! I don't think *he* wants to marry *me*! Why are they being so persistent when it's Norman and me who have to make up our minds?"

Longarm murmured, "Colonel's orders, most likely. I don't know if our mysterious colonel is ignorant of the law or only out to muddy the waters. Did you ever have the feeling things were coming to a head and you still had no idea what those things were?"

She said, "That's silly. How do you know they're about to do something if you don't know what they mean to do, Custis?"

He said, "Time and tide wait for no man, and they've spent weeks at lathering everybody up for some serious riding. You can't just take over a town and sit there making faces at people. They've had your Norman send out invitations to the brawl. Even as we speak the army could be fixing to swing around from Fort Union with field pieces to demand some straight answers."

She murmured, "They told me in Santa Fe that poor Norman claims to have planted infernal devices all around this place!"

Longarm shrugged and said, "That's likely why the army issues field pieces. Once a position's been surrounded by superior numbers, it don't matter what the defenders say about blowing the place up. They had a powder magazine at the Alamo. Some say Davy Crocket blew it up, whilst others say he never did, and that's the point. Once the Mexicans had them surrounded by batteries of twelve-pounders, the Alamo was done for. It wouldn't have mattered whether they blew their fool selves up or let Mexican cannon fire handle the chore."

"Then why are they having Norman write those letters? I can't believe poor Norman has any idea what he's doing!"

Longarm said, "I don't know. Fair is fair, and it's commencing to seem as if our mad bomber may be a victim as well. As I've managed to piece things together, your intended had suffered for some time from the consumption before it got really bad and he dropped everything to come out West, searching for a cure. He found himself doped up in bad company, alternately raging and hoping as his funds must have run mighty low. Boarding in a house of ill repute with a serious drug and liquor problem can get expensive."

Clo looked about and murmured, "But this house and all its expensive furnishings . . . ?"

Longarm said, "Your Norman never paid for any of this. I ain't sure anyone has. A man with a private army can order things on credit."

He let that sink in, then continued. "I suspect this mystery colonel they keep talking about was one of the old pals your Norman wrote to about his chemistry experiments out here. I'm not certain he was on to anything new as he dabbled with chemicals in a certain toolshed here in Gilead. But the colonel knew he'd made heaps of gunpowder from humble materials during the war, and Gilead does seem set up to supply the raw materials for serious explosives. So I suspect the colonel came out here just in time to pay off your Norman's debts and take him on as a sort of staff chemist. Norman MacLennon ain't the mad bomber. If there's any mad bomber at all, it's this mysterious colonel!"

Clo stared across at the group gathered over her Norman on the rug as she said, "I'm so glad. But where is this self-described colonel and what do you think he's really up to?"

To which Longarm could only reply, "I don't know. I can think of a whole lot of devilment a man with a few gallons of nitroglycerine may have in mind for soldiers blue headed for a party he invited them to. But I can't see how he'd show any *profit* from pure and simple murder."

She suggested, "What if he's simply a fanatic who wants to start another war betwixt the states?"

Longarm shook his head and said, "Wouldn't work. I ain't got time to lecture you on the arts of war, but take my word. There's more to a war than blood and slaughter. Wars are fought to bend the other side to some concession. You win a war when the other side agrees to give your side something such as land, a trade deal, or mayhaps just your freedom. So mass murder for the sake of mass murder ain't war, it's madness, and I just can't see all these birds in dress gray following a raving lunatic. There has to be some *method* to this madness!"

The JP from town, finding himself ignored, drifted over to join them, asking if they had any idea what was going on.

Longarm spotted the King James Bible the older man was holding in one hand as he replied, "The groom seems to be feeling poorly. I want both of you to listen tight. A marriage ceremony ain't binding if it's not entered into willingly by all concerned. So just go along with this charade and you have my word I can have it annulled in a federal court, if ever we get out of here alive. Could I have a look at that Good Book you're packing, pard?"

As the JP handed over the Bible, Clo told him, "We think somebody around here might be touched in the head. It may not be my poor Norman after all!"

She went on talking to the older man as Longarm leafed through the Old Testament, cutting in to ask, "Do you recall that street address the professor gave you, Miss Clo?"

She thought, nodded, and said, "By heart. I've read the poor dear's letters over and over. He told me to see someone named Sam at number 822 Jeremiah Street. Why do you ask?"

Longarm said, "I ride for Uncle Sam, and he might have meant us to look up Jeremiah, Chapter Eight, Verse Twenty-two, because that puts a whole new light on this whole shebang!"

Before he could explain further, Old Sarge called, "We're ready now!" By then the others had Professor MacLennon back on his feet, sort of. Old Sarge said, "Get over here and let's get cracking. I'm hungry!"

Then Professor Norman MacLennon shook himself free and staggered to the fireplace to lean against the marble mantel with one elbow as he took something from his coat pocket with his free hand.

Holding up what seemed like a fifth of gin, Norman MacLennon snarled, "Leave me the fuck alone! Get your fucking hands offa me! Do you see what I got here, you fuckers? Do you know what's in this bottle?"

It got very quiet as Old Sarge softly said, "We know what you have there, Professor. Why don't you hand it over easy now."

The consumptive chemist snarled, "Suppose I don't? Suppose I drop it on this flagstone hearth, you high-and-mighty enlisted fuck?"

Old Sarge looked as if he was having a bad dream and trying hard to wake up as he pleaded in a desperately calm voice, "You don't want to do that, Professor. We're all friends here, see?"

The professor coughed, stared owlishly at Longarm and his intended, and croaked, "Get her out of here! Do it now!"

But Clo tried to go to him as Longarm held her firmly by one arm and told the JP, "Grab the other and let's do as the man says."

Old Sarge protested, "Hold on! I never said anyone was leaving!"

But Longarm and the JP kept easing Clo backward as the professor wildly waved his gin bottle and flared, "Get the fuck out of here with her!"

Clo sobbed, "I can't leave you, Norman! Won't you let us help you?"

The consumptive chemist managed a smile that hinted at the handsome young man he'd once been as he told her in a more rational tone, "I fear nobody can help me now, dear heart. But I'll feel better about my bitter fate

135

if you'll be kind enough to get out of here and have a nice life!"

He added, "Don't any of you other fuckers move!" as Longarm and the JP led Clovinia Cullpepper out into the hall and almost carried her out the back way.

In the dark backyard they were challenged by a voice calling out, "Moon over the Mississippi." So Longarm called back, "Mississippi moonbeams," as he moved closer ahead of the others.

The sentry asked, "What's going on inside? I heard somebody yelling. Is the professor drunk again?"

Longarm calmly replied, "I reckon," as he swung hard and decked the sentry with the butt of his six-gun.

He bent to disarm the Texican, and handed the weapon to the older JP as he rose, saying, "Let's move it on out. Where's the nearest horse and buggy?"

The JP said, "Livery stable down the way, I reckon. But I ain't leaving my wife and daughter!"

Longarm told him to suit himself, and steered Clo straight down the path along the north side of the property. As they moved along alone in the dark, she asked where he was taking her.

He said, "Santa Fe. Quickly. They're likely to fan out across town after us. So let's not be in town no more."

As they crossed Main Street to jog along the railroad's coal yard, Clo asked, "On foot? All the way to Santa Fe on foot through the desert? You can't be serious!"

He assured her he was, adding, "It ain't but twenty miles or so and the night is young. We can make her before daybreak if we walk all the way. But I doubt we'll have to."

He led her across the tracks into high chaparral as she wailed she was wearing high heels.

He said, "We'll circle back to the tracks where the footing will be firmer, once we're out of earshot of that dispatch shed. At least one confederate of the colonel works for the railroad. They've been getting news from the outside world along the railroad's telegraph line. I suspect it's somebody working in the Santa Fe yards. I hope I'm right. I sort of like old Pop up this way."

The going was too tough for much more conversation before they'd circled wide to move back on the narrow-gauge right-of-way south of town.

The cross ties and gravel ballast between the rails spaced three feet apart were a vast improvement. So Longarm urged Clo on for a mile or more before he called a halt.

The confused blonde sank down to perch her shapely derriere on a trail as she sobbed, "Thank God! I don't think I could have managed another step!"

Longarm stared soberly back at the distant winking lights of Gilead as he told her, "Might not have to. Sit tight whilst I shinny up a telegraph pole."

But she rose again as he proceeded to do so, calling up to him, "What do you think you're doing? You can't send a telegraph message from up there, can you?"

He called down, "It's been done. But I don't want any more messages moving along this line."

He hooked an elbow over the crossbar, fished out his pocketknife, and slowly but surely sawed through the softer copper wire with a blade that was sure to need fresh honing now.

As the severed wire twanged loose and fell across the chaparral down below, Longarm descended to tell Clo, "What I just done won't tell 'em as much as any message I could have sent. The line could have gone down by accident. Railroads don't run without a telegraph assuring 'em. So as soon as they notice in Santa Fe, they'll close the line to traffic and send a repair crew out. That colonel can't have *everyone* in the Santa Fe line on his secret payroll. So as soon as they show up, we can pop out of the sticker-bush and ask them for a ride into town."

Clo started to ask why they'd want to hide out in the chaparral to wait. But her travels were broadening her fast. So she nodded gravely and said, "If those ruffians come down this track in search of us, it might be best if they couldn't *see* us. But all those thorny bushes make me uneasy just walking through them. Do you think there might be snakes and such out yonder in the dark?"

He took her by one elbow to steer her from the track as he gently replied, "Snakes are the least of our worries right now, ma'am."

It might have worried her needlessly to remark that the first few hours after dark were, in fact, the chosen dinnertime of the western diamondback. With any luck your average rattler would slither out of the way of any critter too big to swallow whole.

He figured they'd been gone from that Pedersen place a little over half an hour by then. But if Old Sarge had regained the upper hand, he didn't seem to be raising any hue and cry.

It was hard to see much by the dark of the moon. But when he sensed they were in a sandy wash, Longarm told Clo, "It ought to be safe for us to sit down out here. We'll be able to hear anybody on our side or the other moving along yonder tracks. But they'll have no call to look for us here."

Sinking gracefully to the sand, Clo said, "Praise the Lord. Every time I say I can't go another step, you make me go another step. What do you think Norman had in that bottle he was threatening to drop on the hearth, Custis?"

Longarm replied, "They thought it was nitroglycerine. So he must have been making some, out of thin air or in some old-fashioned way."

"He was acting so strange!" she marveled. "As if he didn't really know what he was doing!"

Before Longarm could answer, the sky to the northeast

lit up and then they heard a thunderous echoing roar.

"What was that?" Clo asked as things still seemed to be coming down all over Gilead.

Longarm said, "It *was* nitroglycerine, and your Norman knew *exactly* what he was doing, Miss Clo."

# Chapter 16

Longarm didn't know and couldn't say just what had happened back in Gilead. A test tube of pure nitroglycerine had about the bang of a full stock of dynamite. So from the sound of things, they'd had the professor messing with lots more in that very same house. Not knowing how many might have lived through the blast, Longarm and Clo sat tight in that wash for the next hour or more.

Being a woman confused, Clo likely confided more in him, alone in the dark, than she might have at a Sunday-go-to-meeting-on-the-green. She said, "You don't think I could have . . . caught any social disease from Norman, back in Charleston, do you? I mean, we only . . . did it the night we became engaged, last autumn."

Longarm calmly assured her, "Not likely in Charleston, ma'am. They say he only got to acting really wild after he came out here for his health and made himself sicker on laudanum."

She dabbed at her eyes and declared, "I never would have given in at all if I'd known he was going to go crazy and scare people so. But he must have cared for me a little, don't you think? I mean, he did make them let us go, and that has to count for something!"

Longarm grimaced and said, "I'd say you counted a lot to him, Miss Clo. Even out on his feet, he was doing his best to look out for you."

"Do you think they're liable to hurt him now that we've gotten away?" she asked.

Longarm said, "I hope I'm wrong. But I don't reckon anyone can hurt him now, ma'am. You were right about him all along, and the rest of us were as wrong. Norman MacLennon wasn't a bad man. He was a dying man, and he knew he was dying, and that got him to railing and flailing a mite. But when really bad men tried to use him for their own wicked ends, he tried to warn us, even as they forced him to write threatening letters."

She said, "I told you I didn't have another beau at 822 Jeremiah Street. What was the secret message from the Good Book, Custis?"

He answered truthfully, "Ain't as certain now as I was a few minutes ago. I got to study on it some more. But suffice it to say, your intended was neither the ringleader nor a willing party to the machinations of that mysterious colonel."

When she allowed she couldn't think of any former Confederate pals of her Norman Longarm said, "Don't have to be somebody the profesor wrote directly about his newfound noisemaking powers. Suffice it to say, this self-styled colonel discovered a half-crazed chemist in a town just made for making nitroglycerine, and headed out this way to muscle in."

Help finally arrived from Santa Fe in the form of a work train shoved up the track by that same narrow-gauge Shay. Knowing there could be trouble out Gilead way after hearing about that mad bomber, some county deputies had ridden the flat car out, and better yet, had Winchesters to spare.

So Longarm sent Clo back to the city with the telegraph crew, and led the four other lawmen on foot along the tracks. By this time there was plenty of torchlight up ahead as the people of Gilead gathered around what was left of the old Pedersen place.

There wasn't much. The thunderous blast under the mansard roof had flattened the house into its foundation and set the splintered wood on fire. The Gilead fire volunteers had felt no great call to put the fire out.

Most, although not all, of the servants had made it out alive. Like Longarm, Clo, and the JP, they'd backed off while Professor MacLennon held Old Sarge and the others at bay with his private stock of nitroglycerine. It wasn't as clear whether anyone else had made it out in time, or just what had gone wrong in the end. There was nothing to be seen of the professor, Old Sarge, or even that marble fireplace mantel now.

So now it was the turn of any surviving members of the colonel's private army to hide out around Gilead as Longarm, the county law, and a deputized posse of pissed-off townsfolk searched for evidence.

They failed to find enough to matter. There were some work benches and a big cast-iron kitchen range up the slope in the front of that abandoned bat cave. You could smell the headachy fumes of nitroglycerine, along with bat shit, in the fetid air up yonder. So they'd been fooling with it in the caves. But any serious lab shit for making any sort of acid seemed to have gone up with the house. MacLennon's secret lab setup appeared to have been up inside that mansard roof atop the pile. They'd only *tested* the results up in the caves. That accounted for both the remaining fumes and the way the ground had shaken whenever they'd set a batch off. The still-burning ruins warned one and all against setting one batch of nitroglycerine off too close to another.

A local man familiar with the smell and conversant with blasting said the professor would have been safer making his hellish brew into dynamite. Longarm knew this, but heard him out politely.

The man said, "It ain't hard. Many a man wished he'd thought of it first after Mr. Nobel in Sweden saw you only had to mix nitroglycerine with clay and wrap waxed paper around it. We use dynamite up the line all the time and it hardly ever goes off by accident."

Longarm said, "Some crooks use the liquid for special jobs, such as blowing safes. Do you shoot the pure bang juice into a lock, or along a waxed-in door seam, and then slam the safe sudden with a sledgehammer, the sharp detonation, right where you want her, can open a safe like a sardine can."

"Don't them safecrackers have to be mighty careful?" asked the bat-shit blaster.

Longarm dryly remarked, "Yep. But looking on the bright side, it often saves the state the expense of a trial."

Someone asked about those rumors of hidden demijohns or tanks of nitroglycerine, rigged with tricky fuses, in and around Gilead.

Longarm said, "There's nothing tricky about an acid fuse. Suddenly mix sulfuric acid with most anything that will burn and you get a heap of sudden heat. But the more I think about it, the surer I feel I'd set a dynamite cap with a sprung trigger to detonate nitroglycerine."

"You mean that was all a big bluff?" a county man demanded.

Longarm said, "I'm still working on that. There surely was at least a demijohn of the real thing over to the Pedersen place. It's way more important to catch up with the mysterious colonel and any survivors than to tally up their ordnance!"

So they searched, and searched, and not finding anybody, didn't know if there were any survivors or not. A crook in hiding is by definition a crook you can't question.

So Longarm borrowed a pony and rode back to Santa

Fe in the wee small hours. Getting in before dawn and not wanting to pester anybody, he went to Tess Bronson's place by the river, and she didn't mind at all.

He'd forgotten how pretty her mousy brown hair hung down over her tits by candlelight, after being with the tawny Consuela and the older and rustier Penny Brite.

After an hour's sleep alone in her bed at last, Longarm ambled on into the plaza and, Tess being busy in the Hall of Records, spent the rest of the morning sending wires and consulting with local lawmen and Lieutenant Lowell from the Provost Marshal's Office.

It was Lowell who told him two squadrons of cavalry out of Fort Union were on their way, with the reserve squadron and post operating troop perforce left to hold the fort.

Longarm said, "Aw, shit, I was afraid of that! Where would they be right now and how can I hope to get in touch with 'em?"

The first lieutenant said, "Nobody can get in touch with that column at the moment. They're on the trail down the far slopes of the Sangre de Cristos to Las Vegas. They mean to board the AT&SF at Las Vegas and ride the rest of the way here by rail. So you could wire a message to my opposite number in Las Vegas and they'd get it when they rode in this evening."

Longarm grimaced and said, "Sure I could, with reason to suspect that mystery colonel has at least one confederate monitoring the telegraph lines in these parts! There has to be a better way."

Lowell said, "We could send a dispatch rider along the trackside service road. He'd beat the afternoon eastbound by at least half an hour. Who do you think this apparently rich master criminal you call the colonel has listening in on the wires?"

Longarm said, "If I knew I'd arrest him. Your point about a rich master criminal is well taken. Most crooks take up a life of crime to *take* money, not to *spend* it. So far, we know this unreconstructed rebel, if that's what he is, has paid off the debts of a wild-spending drunken chemist, recruited at least the cadre of a cavalry troop, and outfitted them with half-ass uniforms. He must be paying his informants spread from hither to yon as he keeps tabs on the rest of us, so . . . Right, he has money to burn, or he's in debt to his eyebrows by now!"

The army man asked, "How do you like a rich eccentric playing soldier with his own private regiment? Doesn't your Silver Dollar Tabor up in Leadville own his own Highland regiment in kilts?"

Longarm smiled at the picture and replied, "You're talking about a marching band old Silver Dollar keeps on hand for parades and such. A private army willing to *fight* for you would cost more, and after that, you'd have them *fighting* for you, not just strutting about in dress gray, so . . . You say there's an afternoon eastbound that can get me to Las Vegas before that cavalry column boards a westbound?"

Working for the provost marshal, Lieutenant Lowell was paid to know about such matters. So he nodded and said, "They may beat you in to Las Vegas, but they can't board any westbound before your eastbound clears the single track through the mountains, can they?"

So Longarm went to check the timetable at the railroad depot. He didn't buy a ticket. He knew he could bum a ride at the last minute, and he didn't know who the colonel had watching in the city. He confided those suspicions to Undersheriff Taylor over a glass of suds at the depot taproom, and the local lawman allowed they'd have the rascal in time. It had to be somebody new, or some older railroader who'd suddenly started spending more than usual.

Having done all he could for the moment, Longarm

146

ambled over to the hotel to make sure Clo Cullpepper was all right.

Penny Brite from Gilead caught up with him in the lobby to demand some answers fast.

She said, "I just read about that explosion out at the Pedersen place! Thanks for talking me out of staying there with you! Now you owe me an exclusive on the mad professor blowing himself and all his cohorts up with nitroglycerine!"

So, not wanting any others listening in as they seemed to be about to gather a crowd, Longarm went on up with Penny to her room on the floor above Clo, and it sure beat all how tempting a rusty redhead could be after a morning tub with a mousy gal built entirely differently.

As he went at her dog-style while explaining the events leading up to the dying chemist's self-sacrifice, Penny arched her spine and said, "I know what I said about this only being a passing fancy. But I'm glad to see you didn't waste any of this on that young blonde!"

Gripping a bare hipbone in each hand as he thrust sincerely, Longarm gallantly replied, "You have my word I never even kissed Miss Clo in the process of saving her from a bad marriage."

Penny purred, "I know. I can tell you've been saving all this for little old me. How long are you going to be here in Santa Fe now that you've solved your case?"

He started to say he hadn't even begun to solve shit. But he held his tongue and shoved his old organ-grinder deeper as he truthfully told her, "Not long. Fixing to catch the eastbound AT&SF this afternoon."

So she said she wanted to get on top to give him something to remember her by, and he knew he would, watching her no-longer-young but nicely proportioned torso bouncing above him in broad daylight that way.

Sharing a smoke, Penny confided that she'd landed a job with a paper there in Santa Fe, and meant to sell her printing business in Gilead and move into the big city. He agreed that since they were both going to be busy for the next few days, it might be best if he got on top before he left.

Kissing Penny a fond farewell in her hotel doorway, with her half out in the hall stark naked, Longarm started down the stairs, then cut back up to rap on Clovinia's door.

When she opened it, wrapped in a blue silk kimono against the noonday siesta coming fast, Longarm told her, "I've got to beat the army to Las Vegas, over on the Pecos to the east. I'd be proud to carry you that far, free, unless you have other fish to fry here in Santa Fe."

She smiled up at him wistfully and replied, "I don't have a soul here now. But my things, out there in Gilead . . ."

Longarm said, "You don't have nothing in Gilead if it was in that Pedersen place when your Norman blew it to burning splinters, ma'am. But I can spring for such unmentionables as a lady might need to get back to Charleston from Las Vegas. The train we'll be catching will be going on through. So if you give me a list, I'll be proud to shop for you in the few minutes left this side of noon!"

Clo blushed and protested, "No, thank you very much! There are some secrets a lady likes to keep to herself!"

Then she looked away and murmured, "I suppose, last night, in the darkness and confusion of my mind, I must have given away some things I shouldn't have."

Longarm smiled down at her and mildly replied, "If you did, I just don't recall 'em, Miss Clo. Like you said, we were both shook up from our narrow escape from that exploding house. Do you reckon you could last without a change of unmentionables as far as, say, Kansas, where you'll get to lay over betwixt trains?"

She allowed she could. So he said he'd come back to fetch her when it came time to board that eastbound.

As he turned to go, she murmured, "Bless you, Custis Long. You're a gentleman of the old school despite your country ways. For to tell the truth, I was half expecting you to . . . try and take advantage of my foolish confessions last night."

To which he sincerely replied, "I wouldn't want to disappoint a lady of quality, Miss Clo."

# Chapter 17

Thanks to the wonders of modern science, a hard night's cavalry push took a little over two hours by rail. But that was a long enough train ride for the conversation to dwell once again on the subjects most interesting to healthy young adults with nobody else to talk to. So parting was really sweet sorrow when their eastbound stopped at Las Vegas and Longarm just had to get off. For before she'd let him go, Clo planted a tender parting kiss on his lips and allowed she would never forget him.

The gents who drew maps insisted the main stream of a river was as far upstream as you could trace its furthest branch. So the official Pecos River commenced as a whitewater mountain brook just east of that Glorieta Pass, and then swung east to form the official lower limits of the Sangre de Cristos, before it joined up with the shorter but wider Gallinas north of Santa Rosa. The many springs in or about Las Vegas fed the Gallinas and hence the upper Pecos Valley no matter what the mapmakers said, and Longarm didn't care one way or the other. He found the two squadrons from Fort Union resting up from their hard day's ride near one of those springs as they waited for that westbound to save them another hard ride over the mountains to Santa Fe. The major in command told Longarm they'd brought a battery of Hotchkiss guns, and meant to march on to Gilead as soon as they recovered from a restful train ride.

Longarm explained the way things now stood in Gilead, and headed for the Western Union to get off some wires. Then, seeing he had time, he made a few other calls around the fair-sized railroad town, and got back to the troops from Fort Union as their westbound AT&SF arrived.

So within the hour an Anglo-dressed Mexican had joined a poker game in a back room of a certain Las Vegas saloon to tell a player wearing a white planter's hat, "Things went just the way you said they would, Colonel. The bluebellies from Fort Union are headed over the Sierra with all their pretty ponies and fine popguns! You want me to round up the rest of the boys?"

The colonel, as he was called by his literal confederates, shook his head and chided, "Patience, my child. You must learn not to be too hasty. It will take that troop train hours to roll into Santa Fe. After that, we want to let our soldiers blue ride out across the chaparral a ways, where none of them can hear any messages zipping over their heads along that railroad wire. We dasn't make our own move this side of midnight. So grab a bite and get some rest while the night is young. We'll have some serious riding of our own to manage before dawn catches all those troopers way the hell out of our hair!"

The lookout left. The game continued. The colonel never played draw poker with strangers. So every man there was in on his devious plans for the banks of Las Vegas.

But one of the younger plotters had to show off his limited grasp of guerrilla tactics by saying, "Get there fustest with the mostest, eh, Colonel? By the time them soldiers blue find there's not a chore for them in Gilead and head back this way, trail-sore and muddleheaded, we'll have cleaned out over this way and lit out with our loot and one hell of a lead on them!"

The colonel shrugged and said, "I'll raise you and call. I'm here to play cards, not to recite my plans. I told you all in the very beginning that I'd get shed of the bluebellies before we took this town over long enough to clean it out."

Another follower at the table said, "You're being too modest, sir. Only a military genius like yourself would have seen how to play on the fears occasioned by that poor loony chemist's threatening letters!"

The colonel snorted, "Why, thank you, Ted. The color brown becomes your nose, and bailing out an old comrade of the Lost Cause was the least I could do when he found out I was growing beef instead of cotton out this way and turned to me for help. Forget poor MacLennon, boys. He served his purpose and now he's dead, along with some good old boys I miss a lot worse. I still wish I knew exactly what went wrong over in Gilead. The little they've put out on the news wires leaves more of the sad story untold than explained so far."

The younger one opined, "I'll bet that Longarm we were talking about had something to do with it. The Mexicans say he's a sneaky devil as once tricked some *rurales* and *federales* into blowing one another up for him!"

The colonel shrugged and said, "Not this time. Not if he's waiting for them soldiers blue in Santa Fe."

So nobody searched for Longarm in Las Vegas that night. Not that they'd have found him. And along about midnight, the gang was ready for the big move the colonel had been planning all along.

Despite its name, the town of Las Vegas, New Mexico Territory, was far more Anglo that the older and hence more famous Santa Fe. Las Vegas had never amounted to much before the coming of Texas cattle from the south

153

and the Anglo freight wagons and later iron horse from the East, where such traffic met up near water, wood, and grasslands. Hence Las Vegas barely observed *la siesta,* and turned in earlier than most Spanish-speaking communities. So the streets were deserted and dark when the self-styled colonel's private army rode in off the range to fan out and hit every bank in town at once.

Each squad of masked riders packed the same safe-cracking kits supplied by their mastermind's late chemist. No more than a sledgehammer, some sculptor's wax, and a horse doc's needle filled with nitroglycerine. Each safe-cracking team had trained for weeks with olive oil until they were sure they could wax the door of a safe, inject nitroglycerine around it, and give her the one good whack the colonel had said it would take. There'd been no call to damage the one big Mosler safe they'd practiced on.

With spring roundup just over and all the big outfits down the Pecos to the border fixing to start their market drives north, the bank safes of Las Vegas figured to be stuffed with extra cash for the cattle barons to borrow or draw on. It took a lot of cash to fund a cattle drive, and a lot of cattle drives were about to get going.

So the would-be bank robbers got going by the dark of the moon in the smug assumption their mastermind had suckered the troops up at Fort Union. And he had, up to a point. But then things commenced to go terribly wrong as the band rode into the plaza near the railroad depot and fanned out to be hit, in turn, by withering gunfire from the dismounted cavalry troopers posted to cover every likely target.

As horses neighed wild-eyed, rearing, falling with their riders, or running off with empty saddles, more than one outlaw yelled, a tad late in the game, "It's a trap!"

So those still able made for their preplanned getaway routes out of Las Vegas. But Longarm and the major had covered them as well with other troopers and those booming Hotchkiss field guns, aimed to chase thundering hoof-beats out across the surrounding range instead of aimed where they might bust some glass in town.

As the guns fell silent for lack of moving targets, the town of Las Vegas awoke as to the dawn, with townsfolk flinging open their doors and windows to gaze out in wonder at the shattered men and horseflesh littering their streets as the smoke haze cleared.

One of the outlaws who'd been shot off his mount was still conscious as Longarm stood above him with a lantern in one hand and a .44-40 in the other. He stared up with a sheepish smile to gallantly admit, "That was right slick of you, Uncle Sam. But how in the hell did all you blue-bellies get off that westbound after we saw you leaving aboard it?"

Longarm hunkered down beside the badly wounded Texas rider to calmly reply, "Same way we got on it, when it wasn't moving. We rode as far as the next stop down the line at Romeroville, and headed on back. We left most of the saddle stock at a Mexican spread a mile outside of town, knowing your mastermind was Anglo. So now I have a question for you. Who did you say that mastermind was?"

The dying outlaw didn't answer. He'd finished dying. Longarm muttered, "Shit!" and straightened up.

His newfound pal, the young major who'd thought he was headed for Gilead, joined him to chortle, "Lord, it really must smart when a Hotchkiss shell goes up your pony's ass and bursts under your saddle. We have really done a job on these unreconstructed rebels, and so far I've counted twenty-three bodies. Human bodies, that is."

Longarm said, "The one I got a few words out of before I found this other dead bastard still breathing agreed their leader was called the colonel and wore a big white planter's hat. Your turn."

The major said, "Not down the line where I legged it

in from. But we know at least a few of them got away. You never get every fish in the barrel. But how far can they hope to get? You wired north, south, east, and west before they rode into our setup. Every lawman in every direction will be on the prod for hard-riding strangers, wounded or not."

"If the mastermind and key leaders are strangers in these parts," Longarm pointed out. "That so-called colonel has been just out of my range of vision since I came down from Denver looking for somebody else entirely. I doubt he could be invisible. He must be somebody folks in these parts don't think of as a stranger. Somebody who *belongs* in these parts when he's wearing his other face."

The young major frowned thoughtfully and asked, "Didn't you tell us this so-called colonel seemed to be heading up a reconstituted Texas Militia, as if he thought he was a latter-day Brigadier Sibley?"

Longarm said, "I did. And as we speak, Uncle John Chisum of the Jingle Bob is one of the biggest cattlemen in New Mexico after coming west after the war from Texas with a herd he never paid for. A heap of us came west after the war for new starts. Folks out our way are inclined to accept you as an old pioneer if you've been out here five minutes longer than they have. As for Texican riders wearing Texican hats and spurs that jingle, you'll find the breed as far north as Wyoming these days, thanks to the Union Pacific and the Goodnight-Loving Trail."

The major said, "Then our mysterious colonel could have simply gone to ground at any spread or in any town in these parts. So what do we do now?"

Longarm waved his gun muzzle expansively and suggested, "See about getting these streets cleared before the kids have to walk to school in the morning. Then I aim to canvass the banks to see which of 'em got hit the hardest just now."

156

The major pointed out, "Thanks to your timely tip, the banks of Las Vegas are in your eternal debt. I doubt many, if any, could have been seriously damaged."

Longarm replied, "That's what I just said. I'll be over at the Drover's Rest across from the depot till banking hours if you need me. Otherwise, I'd like to see if I can catch some sleep. For some reason I'm commencing to feel sleepy-headed."

They shook on it, and would have parted friendly had not they heard an alarm triangle in the distance and somebody closer calling, "Fire! Fire!"

So they stepped further out in the street, around a fallen pony, to see the glow of flames against the sky down to the south. Then a steam-powered pump engine came rattling by, drawn by its eight-man crew of volunteers in red suspenders and leather helmets.

As Longarm and the officer jogged after it, the young major called out, "Where's the fire? What's burning?"

Nobody answered back, but loping along at his side, Longarm called out, "Save your breath. There was a bank down that way. Stockman's First Trust, they called it."

The major asked him how he knew.

Longarm felt no call to answer until they joined the gathering crowd out in front of the flaming Stockman's First Trust before he sighed and said, "Figured they were fixing to do something like this."

Then he moved over to the fire engine, set his lantern on its running board, and looked around for the fire captain.

When he spied the part-time fireman's gilt helmet, he made his way over, elbowing other firemen out of the way to grab the captain by one sweaty sleeve and spin him around, yelling, "Keep your men back from that bank. It might be rigged to blow up!"

The fire captain, who lived in Las Vegas and held his head high there, shook free to exclaim, "Get back and leave us to do our job, you fool! The roof's about to cave in, but with any luck we may still save the contents of the vaults!"

Longarm insisted, "You ain't supposed to. One will get you ten some sneaky son of a bitch put a nitroglycerine bomb in one of the safe-deposit boxes!"

"Get this fool off me!" the fire captain wailed as two of his men came over to grab Longarm's sleeves on either side.

The fire captain yelled, "Henderson, Smithers, train that hose way lower through the front windows and knock them flames *down,* not *up!*"

But Longarm still had his .44-40 in one hand, so he fired it up at the sky, twisted loose in the sudden spell of frozen astonishment, and threw down on the captain, yelling, "Get your boys and your own ass *back* and do it *now!*"

So they did as he commanded, threatening him with twenty years at hard for aiding and abetting arson as the hose crew stubbornly trained their water through the flaming front of the bank, even as they moved backward away from it.

Then there came the thunderous roar and ground-shaking thump you get around mines or quarries at blasting and flaming debris went flying in every direction, with one burning beam missing Longarm and the fire captain by yards.

"Jesus H. Christ! How did you know?" gasped the leader of the local volunteers as his men fanned out without orders to douse the widely scattered glowing embers.

Longarm said, "I'm U.S. Deputy Marshal Custis Long. I've been working on this case a spell, and of late I'm commencing to see how their mastermind's mind works."

The Las Vegas fire captain put out a hand to shake and declared, "You'll never know how glad I feel about that! We heard about you and that mad bomber. He set fire to

158

this bank to lure us close enough to be blown up by one of his bombs, right?"

Longarm didn't have the time—he was starting to feel sleepy again—so he shook with the good sport and answered simply, "Something like that, pard."

# Chapter 18

Longarm figured any city fire marshal worth his salt would read ashes better than your average lawman, and so, seeing the Stockman's First Trust needed some time to cool down, Longarm locked himself away for some serious sleep.

He'd gotten mayhaps four hours of it before there came a thunderous pounding on his hired door. When he opened it, bleary-eyed and gun in hand, a big gruff cuss in a rusty black suit bulled into the room to declare himself Marshal Masterson Sinclair of the Las Vegas District Court and demand to know what the fuck one of Billy Vail's Denver dudes was doing in his jurisdiction.

He added, "I known they call you Longarm and you think your shit don't stink. But where do you get off leading a military expedition through the streets of Las Vegas and ordering our fire volunteers around like this was dammit Denver?"

Longarm tottered back to the bedstead in his long underwear and put his six-gun back in its holster as he answered, "Don't get your bowels in no uproar, Marshal. There wasn't time for a courtesy call and I was never in command of them troops. I only headed 'em off to keep

161

'em from being sent on a wild-goose chase when the action was planned for here in your district. I had no more authority over a local fire company than you would have. But I'm sure you'd have told them if you knew there might be a bomb set to go off in a burning building."

As Longarm moved to the corner washstand, Masterson Sinclair let fly. "Maybe I would have. But what makes you so smart-ass about such matters here in my jurisdiction?"

Longarm began to wipe the sleep out of his eyes with a damp cloth as he patiently replied, "The case didn't commence in your jurisdiction. The mastermind behind the flimflammery never wanted anyone to suspect he had toad squat planned for anything on this side of the Sangre de Cristos. He wanted us to gaze hard upon Gilead, jurisdiction of the Santa Fe District. The marshal over yonder didn't mind. He's busy with other crooks, and somebody in Washington who heard my shit don't stink *asked* me to give them a hand over yonder."

Billy Vail's opposite number in Las Vegas snapped, "Well, this here federal marshal never did. You and them soldiers blue made an awesome mess outside last night, and when them reporters came calling at my door this morning, I couldn't tell them shit!"

Longarm dried his face as he said, "I meant to make the usual courtesy call and let you and your own deputies in on it before I made any arrests, Marshal."

Sinclair thundered, "Bullshit! You ain't about to arrest nobody here in my jurisdiction! Do you have any charges against anybody in these parts as needs arresting, you just fork over their names and me and mine will handle any such chores for Uncle Sam!"

Longarm answered truthfully, "I'm not sure who the mastermind behind all this skullduggery is, Marshal. He's been playing his cards a mite close to his vest. I only figured just in time that his intended targets were over

162

here your way. He's been busting a gut trying to lure the calvary from Fort Union over on the western slopes of the Sangre de Cristos. That was likely so his gang could light off across the open range to the northeast with no serious pursuit. County posses only pursue so far, but calvary keeps coming, thirty or more miles a day on better-than-average mounts, wiring ahead once they cut your sign."

"I reckon we'd have mounted a fair federal posse here in Las Vegas," the local marshal opined.

It would have been needlessly cruel to remind him he'd just said he hadn't known shit until those reporters woke him up. So Longarm just nodded and said, "They likely overrated the calvary. As I was saying, the rascal who planned it all has made a habit of using others for his own ends. He took a half-crazed dying chemist under his wing and promoted him to a mad bomber the army was going to have to do something about. Fortunately, somebody thought to send me first to scout the situation around Gilead."

"Mebbe so, but they never sent you *here*!" Sinclair complained.

Longarm reached for the shirt he'd hung on another bedpost and replied, "The mastermind didn't *want* me here. He had his dupe, the late Professor Norman MacLennon, writing threatening letters and mixing small batches of nitroglycerine up to lure me, or more important to them, the *army,* away from Las Vegas as the big market drives were forming up and the banks had sent East for more cash to cover checks, loans, and withdrawals. He told his recruited raiders they were welcome to all the cash they could carry off, I suspect. From the way things went after that, I figure he was using them as well to pull off his real crime at Stockman's First National."

"Which was . . . ?" demanded Sinclair.

"Getting rid of Stockman's First National, just as he

managed amid all the confusion last night. His body was not to be found amongst the fallen because he never rid at the head of his made-up Texas Militia. Whilst they were hitting other banks all over town, he snuck in on foot to set fire to Stockman's and slip away like the rat he was born."

"What about that bomb later?" Sinclair demanded.

"Safe-deposit box," Longarm explained, buttoning up the shirt and reaching for his jeans as he continued. "Known about Las Vegas by yet another title, or mayhaps with the help of a confederate, he hired a private safe-deposit box, bold as brass, at some earlier date. Once he had a couple of bottles of nitroglycerine locked away like private liquor at a club, with a fused stick of dynamite to set her off, he just had to bide his time, knowing any time the bank caught fire the bank would be all over literally."

I see how that might have worked," the older lawman conceded, but added, "To what purpose? I've heard of blowing a safe. But what would the profit be in blowing up a whole blamed bank?"

"Records," Longarm suggested, sitting down in his faded jeans to haul on his boots. "Banks keep records of monies owed on checking accounts and bank loans. I've reason to suspect our so-called Confederate colonel may be new in these parts. He may have made up the loss of some old plantation with a new cattle spread or mercantile monopoly, like Uncle John Chisum or Major Murphy down Lincoln County way. I don't suspect neither of *them* of events leading up to last night's shoot-out, but say you were a newcomer to New Mexico Territory's new opportunities with more ambition than ready cash. Then say you were in hock up to your eyebrows to the Stockman's First Trust. But all they had to prove this was your signatures on a heap of records in their vaults."

"All right. So much for motive," Sinclair conceded as Longarm rose to stamp his feet and reach for his gun belt.

Then Sinclair asked him, "Where do you think you're going in my jurisdiction, Denver boy? I reckon we can take her from there. All we have to do is ask the gents who work at that bank for a list of serious debtors. Can't be all that many, can't all of that many hail from Texas, and don't matter whether the formal contracts are intact or not. A banker who can't name such a cuss from *memory* ain't much of a banker in this child's book!"

Longarm mildly said he'd been thinking along those lines.

Sinclair said, "Well, you just go on and think away, little darling. Me and my boys don't need your help in making the arrest."

Longarm sighed and said, "Aw, hell, I meant to cut you gents in on the final official report."

Sinclair insisted, "Don't want to be writ up for no *assist*. Want it *all*. It's what I got coming to me, and by Jimmies I shall have it! So why don't you just hop your choo-choo back to Denver and let us worry our own little heads about our homegrown mastermind?"

Longarm allowed he meant to eat breakfast first. So they both went downstairs together, but parted unfriendly out front.

Longarm really meant to have a good breakfast. But first he ambled over to the Western Union to send off some progress reports.

It didn't take long, but he was wide awake and hungry by the time he got to the Harvey Restaurant in the AT&SF depot and ordered his eggs fried over a T-Bone steak cooked rare enough to constitute a minor injury to the cow.

He was dawdling over his mince pie and third cup of black coffee as he flirted with a handsome young Harvey girl when Marshal Sinclair joined him at the counter, looking sweaty, as if he'd been rushing to and fro. Longarm didn't care. Harvey girls got fired if they went out with a customer, and he'd been expecting the burly Marshal Sinclair.

Billy Vail's opposite number said, "Just come from my office after calling at the bank manager at his home. He tells me you dropped by yesterday evening and asked for a list of all his principal debtors."

Longarm nodded and calmly replied, "Asked all the banks in town, as a matter of fact. I told you what I figured might have been the mastermind's real target. I got a shithouse full of bank records up in my hotel room."

Sinclair said, "Nobody owing Stockman's First Trust enough to set the place on fire fits your picture of the mastermind. More than one former Confederate rider out of west Texas has commenced to raise cows in these parts. But none of them funded any recent serious operations with that particular bank, and even if they had, blowing up the bank wouldn't have done your mastermind any good. The bank manager makes everybody sign in triplicate. He keeps one extra set in his private home office, and sends another to their main office in Saint Lou. So what have you got to say about *that*?"

Longarm signaled the waitress as he calmly replied, "In that case you are more than welcome to my copies upstairs. When I'm wrong I'm wrong."

He asked the waitress to fetch another slice of pie and a mug of coffee for his long-lost uncle there.

As she smiled and turned away, Sinclair confided, "There was a wire from Washington waiting when I got back to my office just now. Seems they'd ordered me to stay out of your way and let you follow your hunches. So why don't we just work the case together, pard?"

The waitress being out of earshot, Longarm mildly asked, "Why don't you take a flying fuck at a rolling donut? I offered to cut you in. You told me to let you worry about the case on your own. So worry all alone, on your own, all you like, *pard*."

Of course, there was no way he could lawfully handcuff a fellow peace officer to a Harvey girl. So there was no way Longarm could keep Sinclair from tagging along like a big kid as he headed on over to the fire marshal's office.

The fire marshal was even older than Sinclair, but not half as filled with himself. He seemed grateful to Longarm for saving all those volunteers the night before.

He said, "The fire was started with a coal-oil lamp heaved through a back window. We found what was left of it amid the ashes, and you can read which way the flames danced along the timbers if you know the signs to look for."

Longarm asked if his hunch about a bomb in some safe-deposit box made sense. The silver-haired fire marshal said, "Better than that. We can tell you which box the bomb was planted in. Nobody recalls the Mr. MacLennon who rented a safe-deposit box about a month ago. But what will you bet the name was fake?"

Longarm grimaced and said, "Thanks, Mastermind. I was wondering just when you'd come up with your tricky game of Fairy Chess."

He saw he was confusing the two of them, and quickly added, "Fairy Chess is a chess game with some of the rules set different to make the game more interesting for chess masters with too much spare time on their hands. We know that the so-called colonel took the so-called mad bomber, Professor MacLennon, in tow about the same time he hired that safe-deposit box. He might have had the professor whip him up that bomb most any time, short of yesterday at closing time. Professor MacLennon was inclined to rave on, but he was a chemist, and so he did know how to make nitroglycerine, or come by enough to matter at least. So once our mastermind had Stockman's First Trust set to blow up, he spent the next month trying to sucker the U.S. War Department into sending the troops posted at Fort Union on a wild-goose chase. I'll allow a safe-deposit box hired out to a Mr. MacLennon nobody from the bank recalls sounds like the box the bomb would have been planted in, but how can you be sure, sir?"

The fire marshal replied expansively, "It's not there. The high explosives tore it to sheet-metal confetti, and didn't do the boxes all around it any good. They were torn up or mashed flat in proportion to their distance from the center of the blast. Nothing of their contents was recovered intact, of course. Save for a few melted coins and ruined jewelry, scattered amid the burn ruins, there's nothing left of the bomb or the contents of the surrounding boxes."

"Did the blast polish off bank records farther away from them safe-deposit boxes?" asked Marshal Sinclair.

The fire marshal nodded and said, "Hell, half the bank wound up out in the street. Coins and bullion in the safes were recovered, but all the paper money's gone. That was one mighty thorough arson job!"

The authoritive Sinclair turned to Longarm to ask, "What do you reckon we ought to do now, pard? It seems to me we've about run out of sign here. If they used the name of a crazy dead man to hire a safe-deposit box and plant a bomb in it, I don't see how we're going to trace that particular pattern further, do you?"

Longarm suppressed a yawn and said, "Not from here. Got to study some on what you just described as a pattern. Some poor wayfaring stranger who didn't know the rules set up by a Fairy Chess master might not be able to play him a game for spit. But some of the so-called sneaky moves are starting to make more sense as I study the board. He hasn't been all that clever. A master criminal is a plain contradiction in terms because it's sort of stupid to be crooked in the first place. But he's been flimflamming us by moving his chess pieces in *unexpected* ways, not *impossible* ways. So all I have to do now is figure some *possible* move he don't want me to expect."

# Chapter 19

There was more than one way to skin a cat, and if the mastermind hadn't been out to wipe out a debt to Stockman's First Trust, he'd sure gone to a whole lot of trouble to wipe out *something*. So Longarm got back to the bank books at that banker's house while the comely daughter of the house kept serving him coffee, cake, and eye flutters.

Knowing what you were looking for helped a lot, once that fire marshal had pinpointed the exact safe-deposit box where the sneak had planted his bomb. Longarm figured the intent had been to destroy the contents of another box nearby, and after going over the bank's records and paying a call on a friendly probate court clerk, who steered him to the right law firm, Longarm had narrowed the field to nigh dead-certain, provided he could *prove* toad squat.

Meanwhile, bereft of many former associates and having sense enough to get rid of that white planter's hat, the man who no longer wished to be known as the colonel was playing cards with other associates in an upstairs private party suite at Madam Fandora's house of ill repute just upwind of the Las Vegas stockyards.

Members of the WCTU and other reform-minded

groups pictured places such as Madam Fandora's as catering to the baser instincts of drunken brutes with tobacco and worse and mighty wild women. They did, but Madam Fandora was in business for the money, and had her paying clientele required her girls to play harps and wear halos, they'd have done so. It just so happened that the regulars up yonder that afternoon preferred Havana cigars and five-card stud.

Madam Fandora, in the considerable flesh, was holding court there that afternoon, seeing she was no longer expected to entertain any customers on her back unless they were well hung indeed with a whole lot of cash. She was a junoesque bottle blonde trying to pass for, say, twenty-nine at a considerably advanced state of maturity. But she was a jolly old bawd, as long as one didn't cross her, and the boys sort of enjoyed being allowed to talk that rough in front of a woman with her clothes on, if one wanted to call her cancan outfit clothes.

Madam Fandora was enthroned in the bay window on the far side of the room. A tall youth wearing a black sateen shirt and a brace of Starr .45-25's, cross-draw, stood behind the madam's wicker chair as if to push her, seated, most anywhere she chose to go.

When she spied Longarm darkening the door from the inside balcony, Madam Fandora calmly but firmly called out to him, "This is a private gathering, handsome. How did you ever get by my boys downstairs?"

Longarm modestly replied, "I have my resources, ma'am. I generally load 'em five in the wheel. Like I told your boys downstairs, I'd be U.S. Deputy Marshal Custis Long and I'm here to discuss the recent misfortunes of the late Colonel Fullerton Hawkins, C.S.A."

As he addressed Madam Fandora, he was naturally sizing up the five men seated around the card table between them. All five seemed a mite older than himself and hence as liable to have served in the war as a field-grade officer.

Smiling past them at their gracious hostess, Longarm continued. "I'd have been here sooner, seeing your famous afternoon open house is so popular with leading citizens still all dressed up after business hours. But I had a time scouting up court clerks, lawyers, and such who could help me make up my mind exactly who I wanted to arrest over here."

Madam Fandora demanded, "What are you talking about? Nobody can arrest Colonel Hawkins now. He's dead. Died six or eight weeks ago as I recall."

She sighed and added, "I sure wish I could have attended the funeral. He was a Southern gentleman of the old school. Never cheated at cards, neglected to pay a debt of honor, or struck a woman with his hand!"

There came a murmur of agreement from the older men around the table. Madam Fandora said, "I was tempted. The colonel was a widower with no close kin here in the territory, but—"

"You're to be commended for your delicate nature, ma'am," Longarm cut in. "As a matter of fact, the late colonel's closest kin and sole heir would be a daughter, married to a British observer with the Army of Virginia and residing these days in Cork. That's a town in Ireland, not a bottle stopper. The colonel's lawyer here in Las Vegas just told me she and her man are coming to settle his affairs out our way as soon as the Main Ocean calms down some more. The lady is in a family way and prone to *mal de mer*. That's what they call it when you throw up your breakfast on a steamer, *mal de mer*."

What has all that to do with your rude disturbance of our weekly card game, young sir?" asked a heavyset player with a spade beard.

A somewhat younger player in gray verging on lavender nodded and muttered, "Damned right. Sorry, ma'am. One fails to see how the death of even a revered son of the South has any bearing on this sporting event.

It was our understanding Colonel Hawkins died of natural causes earlier this spring."

Longarm nodded and said, "I was just studying his death certificate. His own sawbones was in attendance and the colonel had been feeling poorly for some time. I'm satisfied he died natural. Satisfied I'd never prove otherwise in any court of law."

"Then what is this all about?" demanded Madam Fandora.

Longarm said, "Pure and unadulterated business records, ma'am, as stored in the safe-deposit box of Colonel Fullerton Hawkins, C.S.A., at Stockman's First Trust. I'm sure you all heard about somebody setting the same on fire last night after planting a bomb in another safe-deposit box close to the colonel's. All the others whose boxes were destroyed are alive and mad as anything. Since they have to *say* what they had stored in them other boxes, there's no mystery as to what other boxes might have been the intended target. A friendly clerk as rides herd on papers for the probate court just told me nobody can, or could, get into the late colonel's safe-deposit box before his one heir arrives and his estate gets probated. That's what they call it when the powers that be allow you to collect on a will, probating."

"Then nobody can say what might have been in poor Fullerton's box?" asked the one with the spade beard.

Longarm said, "Nobody but the sneak who blew up a whole bank just to destroy all the dead man's private papers. I was hoping he'd tell me exactly what they were if I managed to take him alive. So I want you all to listen tight."

The one in lavender-gray said, "I confess I had to write an IOU to the colonel after a bad run at cards last fall. But you have my word as an officer and a gentleman that I paid it off as soon as I got my beef check from Chicago!"

Longarm gently but firmly insisted, "That ain't listening

172

tight and that wasn't the sort of confession I had in mind."

When he saw he had their rapt attention, Longarm said, "What I'd like to establish before anybody here gets his bowels in an uproar—sorry, ma'am—is that the man I mean to take back to Denver with me can't be hung by the neck until dead as things now stand. Most if not all of the gents killed so far were on his side, and there's no evidence he ever directly ordered anybody killed outright. Criminal conspiracy? For sure. Arson? No question. But my home office figures, and I agree, that the two owlhoot riders who tried to kill me in turn, over Santa Fe way, were federal wants from other parts who thought I'd trailed them to New Mexico Territory and got too overexcited for their own good. So I want the one of you I'm here to arrest to consider that as I gently place all my cards on my own table."

"You're bluffing," snorted the one with the spade beard. "I see what you're up to and whilst my own heart is pure, I'd advise any old comrade here with anything to hide to just stand pat. His patter is designed to trick a confession from a man he doesn't have a thing on!"

Madam Fandora said, "Captain Ashley is a lawyer."

Longarm ignored them both to continue. "I know for a fact, and I can prove it in court, that the late Colonel Hawkins has a junior partner, another former Texican he left in charge of his day-to-day management of a considerable beef spread down the Pecos."

"A really fine *rancho*," the one in lavender-gray agreed. "They call it the Rocking H, Bar, Lazy H."

"The brand tells the story," Longarm said. "There's a more famous Colorado brand called the Two, Lazy Two, P. You have to say it out loud to get the message. Both partners had the same last initial, H. The junior partner rocked in his saddle some whilst the owner openly lazed on his new veranda with his mint juleps served by free Mexican help instead of contented darkies. Colonel Hawkins made no bones and felt no shame about this. The Rocking H and so forth had been founded with his money. He was rich from before the war, and stove-in too hard by a minié ball to work worth mention *after* the war. So, as you all know, he played here in town a heap whilst his hired help and trusted *segundo* got to work out on the range."

The whorehouse visitor in lavender-gray said, "That, my boy, is the way things are. What point would there be in getting rich if you didn't get to play whilst the working classes worked?"

Longarm said, "The junior partner must have noticed that was the way things were. So he decided to be rich his ownself. It would have been easy to dip in the till whilst your *numero uno* was in town enjoying cards and other pleasures."

He was too polite to comment on the blushing bawd in the bay window.

He said, "You'd only have to lead a few market drives without close supervision to set aside your own bank roll, and since you were the only Anglo allowed at the business ledgers, it would be simple to make yourself more than a junior partner on the books kept out to the ranch house, in one's own room, against the day your despised boss finally played his busted-up self to death."

"Get to the point," the spade-bearded one snapped. "Switching books after the master of the house passed away would be too dangerous to contemplate. How could one be sure there wasn't a duplicate set of books left somewhere else for safekeeping?"

Longarm said, "I'm sure there was. I figure the junior partner was able to determine this by simply asking. Ask a friendly drunk if he feels sure his business records are safe, and he'll likely assure you he has 'em securely stored in a safe-deposit box. So what was a two-faced *segundo* to do when his boss died natural, he replaced the books

174

at the spread, and had no way to get at the books in that safe-deposit box before the dead man's daughter arrived to claim her inheritance? The bank would have a duplicate set of keys, but they'd never let anyone open a dead customer's box before probate, and by then it would be too late."

"Why couldn't the crooked partner use poor old Fullerton's key? He has plenty of time to search for it before any daughter could get here from Ireland!"

Longarm said, "That would be like trying to hide a sore thumb. When you go to unlock a safe-deposit box, an officer of the bank tags along to ride herd on you with his *own* key. You have to put both keys in to open one box. How would you explain what you're doing with a dead man's key before his will's been probated?"

He let that all sink in before he relentlessly continued. "Having contrived to cut himself in for at least half of the daughter's true inheritance, our sneaky *segundo* devised a mighty complicated plan to destroy that safe-deposit box and all the records in it. He knew, as I just proved, that once anyone got to wondering about any one particular scene of destruction, they'd cut his trial as I just did this afternoon. So he dreamed up a wild and woolly scheme to have all the banks in town busted up real bad, and that was his sole reason for all that razzle-dazzle designed to lure the army west of the mountains. He needed to convince a gang of bank-robbing chumps it was safe to rob all the banks in Las Vegas in one night. So he did, and we know how things turned out in one night, and now I'd like Lieutenant Frank Holt, C.S.A., to kindly rise and come along with me!"

Nobody moved. Madam Fandora murmured, "Speed?" and her bodyguard glanced out the bay window behind them. He told her, "More soldiers blue than you could shake a stick at, across the way and surrounding us on the other sides, I'd venture."

Longarm calmly confided, "Just one troop. I could have had more federal deputies, but their boss told me not to pester him. So I never did. Do you reckon you have a dog in this fight, Madam Fandora?"

The hard-eyed whore smiled coldly and declared, "You heard the man tell you to stand up and go along with him, Frank. It's lucky for you he wants to take you in alive. Fullerton Hawkins was a friend of mine."

So Lieutenant Frank Holt, better known as the colonel to his duped recruits, slowly rose from between the spade beard and lavender-gray suit in his own tasteful frock coat of summer-weight seersucker, with a bodacious Le Mat revolver already drawn and trained on Longarm at gut level.

The Le Mat, a favorite with Confederate cavalry officers, was the only revolver chambered for buckshot rounds, and you had to send away to Paris, France, for it.

Longarm let his holstered .44-40 be as he quietly pointed out, "I just told you why I wanted to take you in alive. You may get out, someday, if you come along quiet. Do you kill me, or make me kill you, all bets are off and I'll never speak to you again."

The desperate mastermind in seersucker said, "We're going to do this my way. You're going to turn around and walk downstairs, slow and easy. Then the two of us are going to leave together, like old pals, and do we make it through the stockyards to the back of another address I have in mind, you just might live."

So Longarm shrugged, turned around, and started walking slowly as the erstwhile junior officer circled the table to follow with that deadly Le Mat trained on Longarm's spine.

Then, just as they reached the stairs, a fusillade of .45-25 cut loose behind him, and Longarm crabbed to one side as first more flying lead and then Fullerton Holt went past him. The self-styled colonel tumbled down the stairs after his big Le Mat revolver to wind up at the bottom in a crumpled heap.

Longarm turned to the black-clad bodyguard in the doorway with a smoking six-gun in each hand to say, "I wish you hadn't done that, Speed. You heard me say I wanted to take him in alive."

The gunslick in sateen said, "Heard the boss lady say Hawkins was a friend of ours too. How were you figuring on taking the son of a bitch when he had the drop on you?"

Longarm revealed the derringer palmed in one big fist as he sighed and said, "I figured on just winging him as soon as I had the chance. Now I have to tie up more loose ends on my own, and there may be some we'll just have to go on guessing about!"

# Chapter 20

That turned out about right. Knowing who he was wiring about got Longarm some answers by wire. Folks around Las Vegas who'd know the late Frank Holt as well as the senior partner he'd been cheating tied some other loose ends up. But with Holt dead and most of his more crooked pals dead or scattered, there were just some details it was best to sort of sweep under the rug.

Undersheriff Taylor wired from Santa Fe that they'd gotten a railroad telegraph clerk to confess he'd been passing telegraph messages on to Old Sarge, who'd turned out to be a real lance corporal with General Sibley's column during the war. But Old Sarge had sort of laid it on about standing tall at the Battle of Glorieta Pass. Folks who knew him around San Antonio said he talked a better war than he'd ever fought. But that was fair, when you considered how many old war stories were old bore stories.

By sundown Longarm had pestered everyone he thought he ought to for the day. But he still had some wrapping-up chores, such as the coroner's inquest slated for Wednesday. Like it or not, Longarm was going to testify that the pouty whorehouse tough, Speed Talbot, had been justified in backshooting the late Frank Holt.

So when that evening train rolled in, bound for Santa Fe, Longarm was tempted to take a short ride over the mountains and come back the next day the same way. Madam Fandora just wasn't his type, they fired Harvey girls who got too friendly with diners, and the only maid at his hotel who'd smiled at him was ugly.

But when a man had been lucky at loving or cards, it was smarter to quit while he was ahead. So he was just standing there, admiring the AT&SF Baldwin 4-4-0 as it stood hissing and clanging, when he heard his name called and turned to see Clovinia Cullpepper from South Carolina running at him full tilt.

He caught her as she lept into his arms to throw both her arms around his neck and kiss him like he was a soldier home from the wars and seriously wounded.

When he recovered his balance and they came up for air, Clo cooed, "Oh, Custis, I so hoped you'd still be here!"

To which he could only reply, "I sort of hoped you might come back. There were lots of things I wished for every Christmas that I never got. I see you bought a new dress."

"With new unmentionables," she confided boldly, going on to explain. "I got to do some shopping and some thinking as I laid over betwixt trains in Kansas. Then I caught the next train back to you. Do I have to tell you why?"

He said, "Yep. You're a lady of quality and I am at best free of lice. This ain't going to work, no offense. I'm a knockaround wage earner with a tumbleweed job and, if the truth be known, a heart to go with it. You need some rich gent with honorable intentions, Miss Clo."

She clung to him, insisting, "What are your intentions toward me right this very minute, or is that a tobacco pipe I feel in your pants pocket, you naughty boy?"

He rolled his eyes up to the gathering darkness and declared in a resigned voice, "You can't say I didn't try, Lord."

Then he told her, "Seeing you seem to know so much about pants pockets, where are your bags? We've gone about as far as we can go here in public, and I dasn't take you to the cowhand boardinghouse I've been staying at. But I reckon I can put a double with bath at a way nicer hotel on my expense account, as long as it's understood we ain't going to overdo it. I know what's eating you, Miss Clo. I'd be a liar if I said I didn't want you just as bad right now. But you know and I know this is just one of them things!"

She demurely asked, "Are we going to screw at that hotel, or do you mean to find a tree stump and lecture us all on the dangers of the primrose path?"

So, seeing she'd put it that coyly, Longarm took the shy little gal and her new unmentionables to the Whispering Springs Hotel, where the bedsprings spoke out loud as they made up for lost time.

He discovered to his delight that while Clovinia in the buff was built like a firmer young sister of Tess Bronson, and moved under a man with the warmth of Consuela and the vigor of Penny Brite, she was built nothing like any of them where such considerations really mattered.

It sure beat all how what was in fact some empty space between a lady's legs could be so different every time one changed ladies.

It was likely the lady-stuff that was wrapped *around* each hole in a lady, he decided as she got on top to sort of suck on his old organ-grinder with her thirsty ring-dang-doo. Clo had one of those rare and hence extra-lovable love maws that seemed to fit any size, like a stocking darned with magical yarn, to cling as tight, warm, and wet to every inch of a man's shaft as she slid up and down it, faster and ever faster, until she came so

181

loud he was afraid they'd know what he was up to back in that boardinghouse he'd moved out of.

She cried a lot as he got a cheroot going, kneading one nipple in the dark between the thumb and forefinger of his free hand as he just smoked and waited her out.

So after a while, she sniffed and murmured, "Oh, Custis, I feel so low! Whatever must you think of me now?"

He said, "I think that's about the best lay I've had in a coon's age, and from the way you just laid me, I'd say *you* hadn't been getting any lately."

"I don't know what came over me. Do you know that last night, all alone in the dark on that train, I got to playing with myself? Playing with myself and thinking of *you*, not poor Norman. I confess I'd been wicked with my own hand and fading memories of my intended in the past. But I never caught myself daydreaming about Norman the way I've been daydreaming about *you* ever since you saved me the other night!"

Longarm took another drag, sighed, and said, "Let's be fair. It wasn't me who saved you from whatever they thought they were doing back in Gilead. It was your Norman, who must have really cared for you, Miss Clo."

She sighed and reached absently for Longarm's soft but love-slicked appendage as she said, "I guess so. But he spoke so wild and dirty and he looked so awful that I hardly knew him and it was hard to believe I had ever . . . really kissed him."

Longarm blew a smoke ring in the dark, or thought he might have. Smoking in the dark wasn't as much fun. He said, "The professor wasn't himself. He hadn't been himself since he'd discovered he was dying and lit out for the wide-open spaces, too terrified and drugged up on that mixture of alcohol and opium to think straight."

"Is that why he did all those awful things?" she asked, toying with Longarm's foreskin.

Longarm said, "I just told you he didn't *know* what he

182

was doing half the time. He'd come halfway to his senses now and again and try to remember he was a chemistry professor. He set up a laboratory in a toolshed that might have made a high school boy laugh and mailed out boasting letters, promising or threatening to make valuable nitric acid out of thin air."

"Didn't he?" she asked.

Longarm said, "Not hardly. They've made a few drops that way with high-voltage arcs shot through steam and compressed air. But Mr. Edison says it would take more power than he can produce in all of New Jersey to make enough nitric acid to matter."

He hesitated and then, since fair *was* fair, confided, "Norman was a fair chemistry teacher. He was never an inventor. Showing Confederate ordnance men how to leach saltpeter out of well-rotted crud was no invention. It was a long-established dirty job around castle cesspools or islands covered with too many birds. He showed them how to do it right for mass production. He never discovered nothing *new*."

"Then why did he write those awful latters?" she demanded.

Longarm said, "The first ones were likely no more than the ravings of a desperate man, flailing for help the way a drowning sailor grabs at straws. One of them got to an ordnance officer he'd known during the war. Despite his self-glorification, Frank Holt never saw action and was discharged as a second lieutenant. But he thought your Norman was a chemist of quality, at least at first. Holt had little higher education and he was one of those prickly proud Southerners, the backbone of the Confederate officers' corps, who never had the money to own a fifteen-hundred-dollar slave but were willing to fight to the death for their right to own one if ever they could *afford* to."

She chided, "Don't talk mean about the Lost Cause. There were other considerations, and I was proud of Norman's contributions when he told me about them. I was too little at the time to know about gunpowder."

Longarm dryly remarked, "Jefferson Davis didn't know much about gunpowder and he'd been Secretary of War under Buchanan. The late Frank Holt must have thought a college professor was the bee's knees. So when he found out your Norman was out this way, sick and broke, he got cracking. But I've gotten ahead of myself. So let's go back to a smallholding second lieutenant sent home flat broke from a defeated army."

"Why did he call himself a colonel?" she asked, plucking idly at Longarm's virility.

Longarm said, "Because he'd headed West for a whole new start. He decided he'd been a dashing cavalry colonel when he wasn't drinking with old comrades who knew him. One of these was the late Fullerton Hawkins, C.S.A., a real colonel who would have despised the likes of Brigadier Sibley and his glorified bank robbers. But there were still some of them around, flattered by the attentions of Colonel Hawkins, C.S.A., and whilst all this was going on, his senior partner and true owner of the Rocking H, Bar, Lazy H up and died. That's when Holt started using your Norman as a mad bomber to lure the army over to the far side of the Sangre de Cristos."

He outlined the plot he'd foiled the night before while she'd been jerking off about him. Then he said, "Norman likely told Holt it was possible to make nitroglycerine from acid and fertilizer. He never told him how. He might not have *known* how. He surely didn't have the wherewithal to produce the tons of it they were bluffing about. All that razzle-dazzle with the rendering and fertilizer plants over in Gilead was all bluff. Their secret ingredient was dynamite from the guano operations up the line. They used the old safecracker's trick of soaking dynamite in hot water stick by stick. Inert clay settles to the bottom. The oily nitroglycerine floats to the top and you skim it off, careful as all get-out."

She kissed his bare belly as he explained, "Holt got your Norman to write wilder and wilder letters. But as the professor proved the other night, there was still some manhood aboard a sinking ship. So he took to slipping coded messages for us in some of his letters. Nobody urging him to threaten the whole outside world was a biblical scholar."

She kissed in the dark where it counted, shyly observing, "I've heard those wicked French girls go farther than this with the lamps lit! I don't recall anything about the Good Book in those letters poor Norman wrote about blowing things up."

Longarm dryly observed, "I would never take you for a Sunday school teacher, Miss Clo. I ain't read the Good Book much either since they let me out of Sunday school. So I missed his clue myself, the more fool me, till I had that chance to look up Jeremiah, Chapter Eight, Verse Twenty-two, when Old Sarge dragooned that Bible-toting J P to marry you up so's you couldn't testify against your Norman or his pals."

She kissed the tip of his rising occasion some more and demanded, "Well, tell me what it *said* so's we can . . . change the subject, darling!"

Longarm said, "I reckon I was no thicker than the Governor. Lew Wallace just published a novel set in Biblical times and the letter your Norman addressed to *him* mentions Saint Thomas as well as the scolding prophet Jeremiah!"

She didn't seem to be following his drift. She might not have been as interested in her Norman's ravings as before. So Longarm told her, "There's more than one Saint Thomas these days. But back when Mr. Ben Hur roamed the Holy Land there was only one Saint Thomas, the one called *Doubting Thomas*, wandering them hills with Jesus Christ the Lord, amen. They called him Doubting Thomas because he wanted to be shown a miracle before he'd believe in one. So as soon as I read Jeremiah, Chapter Eight, Verse Twenty-two, the coded message of a gallant dying drunk was clear as day!"

"Then what did it *say*, darn it? Are you trying to tease me, Custis?"

He laughed, took her by the nape of the neck under her long honey-blonde hair, and answered, "Yep. Jeremiah, Chapter Eight, Verse Twenty-two reads, and I quote, *Is there no balm in Gilead?* And every time he mentions Jeremiah, the professor declares, *That's right!*"

As he pressed her face closer to where he wanted it, Clo pulled it back enough to gasp, "Did you say *balm*, or *bomb*, dear?"

He said, "I doubt your Norman could have meant *balm*. Once I saw he was trying to tell all of us there was no bomb in Gilead, things fell in place. If there was no real threat in Gilead, there was no point in sending the U.S. Cavalry to the rescue over yonder. As I wondered what the same soldiers blue might be posted *closer* to, over here in cattle country with the big outfits shaping up for the summer market drives, it was as if the scales had fallen from my eyes and I could see at last!"

She giggled and said, "That's more than I can say! I can't see a thing in here with the lamp unlit!"

So Longarm snubbed out his cheroot, struck a light, and lit their bedlamp. Then he calmly remarked, "There you go. See anything you like?"

Clovinia Cullpepper didn't answer. She couldn't, with her mouth that full.

Watch for

# LONGARM AND THE WAYWARD WIDOW

266th novel in the exciting LONGARM series
from Jove

*Coming in January!*

# LONGARM

**Explore the exciting Old West with one of the men who made it wild!**